THE THIRTEENTH SANTA - A NOVELLA

THE THIRTEENTH SANTA - A NOVELLA

THE REBECCA MAYFIELD MYSTERIES

JOANNE PENCE

QUAIL HILL PUBLISHING

Quail Hill Publishing

Eagle, ID 83616

Visit our website at www.quailhillpublishing.net

Completely revised from prior editions.

First Quail Hill Publishing Print Book: April 2014

Second Quail Hill Publishing Print Book: August 2018

First Quail Hill Publishing E-book: April 2014

THE THIRTEENTH SANTA - A NOVELLA

1

———————

IT WAS CHRISTMAS EVE and Homicide Inspector Rebecca Mayfield was on a case.

Garlands of silver tinsel and strings of cheery lights decorated the outdoor parking lot of San Francisco's largest mall. In the center of it, while curious shoppers gawked and impatient drivers raged over the loss of parking spaces, yellow crime scene tape surrounded a black body bag. Homicide detectives were put in charge when a suspicious death occurred, and as soon as Rebecca arrived the concerned merchants of Stonestown descended on her, screaming their outrage over the distasteful police presence. A corpse could dampen tidings of good cheer under the best of circumstances, they protested, but to see one at high noon on the day before Christmas would cause shoppers to flee to the competition.

Frankly, surveying the crowd, it didn't appear as if anyone much cared.

Earlier, as she drove to the mall in answer to the SFPD dispatcher's call, she'd worried about the crime scene because of both the day and the location. She hoped the death would have a simple and obvious explanation—bad health, for example.

Joggers, in particular, were big on dropping like flies in the damnedest locations.

Given the strange smirks on the faces of the patrol cops who guarded the body, though, she had the bad feeling that there'd be nothing at all normal about this case.

Officer Mike Hennessy was a friend from the Taraval Station. Like her, he was single and therefore a prime candidate for holiday duty. They'd dated a couple of times until both realized it wasn't going to work. Maybe it was because as a homicide inspector, she was superior to him. Or maybe something else. She didn't know, and preferred not to analyze it.

"What's so funny, Mike?" She pushed back the sides of her black wool blazer, her hands on the hips of her black slacks as she surveyed the area. The air was crisp, the sky pale blue. Gulls swarmed overhead awaiting discarded food from overfed, harried shoppers. "You guys look ready to split your guts about something."

Officer Hennessy's eyes darted toward his partner. His mustache twitched in his effort to keep a straight face. "There's nothing funny, Rebecca. A man's death is never amusing."

His partner sputtered and clamped a hand over his mouth. Rebecca glared. The more he tried not to laugh, the more his shoulders shook.

"You're right, Mike." Rebecca flipped open her pocket notebook. "A man's death is a grave matter."

Hennessy's partner stomped his foot, and doubled over from his struggles.

"Remove the sheet, please," she ordered.

Hennessy carefully lifted it away, reversing the direction he'd placed it over the body to cause minimal disruption to any evidence.

Even being a cop, the sight jarred her at first, then calmly, she studied the victim. He looked like a bloodied, broken rag doll.

His bones were twisted at unnatural angles and his body seemed oddly squished, as if he'd fallen from a great height. She looked up and then all around. They were in an open parking lot. No buildings were near. There was nothing for him to have fallen *from*.

That was when she realized what had amused the cops. Even before Hennessy spoke the words, she could predict what he was going to say. "It looks like"—he began before, like his partner, he sputtered and chuckled—"it looks like he fell off his sleigh."

"He hit the eject button by mistake," his partner blurted.

"Santa the sky-diver." Hennessy howled.

As the two rolled around with laughter, Rebecca made no reply. It was Christmas Eve, and Santa Claus—red suit, tasseled hat, black boots and all—lay at her feet, dead.

"What the hell! This is crazy!" Richie Amalfi stomped back and forth over an empty parking space, gesturing wildly. A short while ago the space was filled by a monstrous white Econoline passenger van. And the van was filled with twelve Very Important People. But now, it—and its passengers—were gone. "I don't believe it!" he bellowed with rage.

Wasn't it bad enough that he, a man who usually saw the light of dawn as he was going to bed, had to face it this morning when he got up? Now, the whole reason he had roused himself at such an ungodly hour had all fallen apart. He should have stayed home. Bed, booze and broads—they were what made life worth living. And his life wasn't going to be worth squat if he didn't solve this present problem.

He ran both hands through his black hair. His eyeballs bulged; his scalp felt like it was being squeezed.

It was nearly Christmas. Filled with good cheer, he had agreed to handle this little task. Now, his Christmas spirit was going to get him a .45 through the brain.

That morning at the San Francisco airport he'd picked up his charges one-by-one as they arrived from different parts of the country. The first was there at seven, the last at ten. The four who had come in from the east coast had arrived the night before and stayed at an airport hotel.

Like some little Mary Sunshine googly-eyed social director he'd gathered them all together, waited while they put on their disguises—lifetimes of paranoia didn't die easy—and squeezed them into the twelve-passenger Ford Econoline van he'd borrowed from a *goomba* for just this purpose.

He'd barely left the airport, on 101 North, when the piece of crap van started to cough and shimmy like a TB victim. He pulled off at the nearest freeway exit. It was just a block from a gas station, so he'd told the passengers to wait while he went for help. Nothing wrong with that, was there? At least he didn't have to go far, dressed as he was in an Armani double-breasted pin-striped suit, white shirt with lots of starch in the collar the way he liked it, a red tie, and brand new wing-tipped shoes.

He'd had to wait about twenty minutes for the station's mechanic to finish up with one customer, even though he'd tried to slip the guy a C-note to ditch the earlier job. It could have been a lot worse, though. The day before Christmas, every housewife, Sunday driver, and certifiable moron who should never be allowed behind the wheel of a moving vehicle got on the road to clog it up and call for help when they couldn't figure out how to get the car out of "Park." Bah, humbug! When he saw he'd have to wait for the mechanic, he'd tried AAA, but the phone line was so jammed up he was left on hold and couldn't even get through to an operator.

The day had not started out the way he'd expected, to put it mildly.

And it had just gotten worse.

"It's a van!" he yelled at the bored mechanic. "A huge mother! It can't just disappear."

The mechanic leaned against the tow truck and chewed on a toothpick. "Maybe this is the wrong street?" His manner was so lackadaisical, his tone so condescending that Richie was ready to take the toothpick and shove it down his throat.

But then he thought ... maybe the jerk-off was right.

Not that he forgot where he left the van, but that his passengers might have gotten it going again and test drove it a little way. Yeah, that was it. Hadn't he heard that Joe Zumbaglio used to be called Joey Zoom because he was so good with cars? Although, if it was good at fixing them or at heisting them, Richie couldn't remember.

He rubbed his forehead, then disgusted, flung himself into the truck and directed the mechanic which way to go. Then he directed him another way, and another, until they ended up driving all over the neighborhood, up and down side streets, checking out driveways, back alleys, even along the freeway.

Nothing. No van. No passengers. Only a snickering mechanic.

A small bead of perspiration broke out on Richie's brow. *This isn't happening to me.*

They returned to the gas station and he peeled a fifty off his roll of greenbacks for the driver, the whole time trying to figure out what the hell to do next. He checked the time on the platinum Rolex on his arm. It was a little after noon. He had plenty of time. All day, in fact. No reason to panic.

He paced. He would call a cab, go home and get his car. Yeah, that would work. And while he was at it, he'd make a few phone calls. Just call to say hello, right? And for sure, somebody would say to him, "'Ey, Richie, you won't believe what I just saw."

It wasn't as if he could actually tell anyone what had happened, not if he wanted to see Christmas Day. San Francisco Bay was too close by, and he was allergic to concrete overshoes.

~

Homicide was completely, painstakingly empty. Space-vacuum kind of empty. No telephone rang. No important memos waited to be read. Not even an impersonal interoffice e-mail arrived wishing her a "happy winter season."

A little sad, a little lonely, maybe a little sorry for herself for being stuck here at work instead of with her family for Christmas, Rebecca leaned back in her chair and put her feet up on her desk. She had always wanted to do that. She tapped the eraser end of her pencil against her desk, and watched it bounce. Even the new man in her life, Greg Horning from Vice, had gone back to Cleveland to spend the week with his family.

She sighed. "Jingle Bell Rock" went through her head although she didn't like the song. Then a Snickers bar called her name, and she made her third trip to the candy machine. She slid in a dollar bill.

The machine burped, and the bill slithered out again. She shoved it in; the device up-chucked and spit it back. The junky contraption looked like it was sticking its tongue out at her, daring her to try once more.

She did; same result.

Grabbing the dollar, she returned to Homicide to check her e-mail yet again to see if CSI or anyone else had contacted her. They hadn't.

Not only was Homicide a barren wind tunnel, so was the

entire fourth floor of the Hall of Justice. Even the women's bathroom. Heck, she could have used the men's room if she'd wanted. No thank you.

Lieutenant Eastwood, head of the division, had given everyone the day off except for Rebecca and her partner. It wasn't that Eastwood was being generous; he knew nothing got done on Christmas Eve. Past years, when the staff came in, they fretted about last minute shopping yet unfinished, then went down to the third floor to drown their sorrows with Christmas cheer in the district attorney's office. The punch was so strong, Rebecca was sure the only fruit in it was an orange dipped twice then discarded. Christmas wasn't the time of year a lot of homicides occurred anyway. That was New Year's. All of Homicide would be on duty next week.

She glanced over at her partner's empty desk. Good ol' Bill Never-Take-A-Chance Sutter. He was a snail on the slow road to retirement. With enough time in to collect a pension, he was merely hanging around until he felt "ready" to officially leave. He'd probably show up around three o'clock today, leave at three-thirty. Or sooner. Rebecca wondered if he ever would retire. Generally, a person needed something to retire *from*.

Frankly, it didn't matter if Sutter was here or not. Except for the weird death this morning, all was quiet. Too quiet. She tried to rouse someone from the Coroner's office to do the autopsy on Santa Claus right away, before they went home or visited the DAs, but so far her calls went unanswered. If no one was willing to do the autopsy today, she'd have to wait until December 26th for the results. Not even the coroner was ghoulish enough to do such a procedure and then go home and carve up a Christmas goose.

She rifled through the reports of the few eyewitnesses at the mall. Everyone denied seeing or hearing anything. No one even knew how long the body lay in the parking lot before a harried shopper bothered to report it. The security camera covering that part of the lot had been awaiting repair for the past six weeks.

All she could do now was wait.

Wait for the fingerprints to run through the system, wait for photos of the victim, wait to use them to scan criminal records for digitized matches. She was tired of waiting, and couldn't help but wonder if the dead Santa had a family who was also waiting —waiting for him to return home.

He looked old, like he could be someone's grandpa. What kind of Christmas would his family have once they learned he was dead?

She'd never forget the first time she had to inform a family on Christmas that the husband and father wasn't coming home again. It was horrible. She shook off the memory. She was a cop; she knew death didn't stop for holy days.

The multi-volume California Penal Code lined the book-shelves behind the secretary's desk in the reception area, kept there both because it was huge and also so it wouldn't get lost in the piles of papers around the inspectors' desks. The way the mall's management had pushed her to shut down the crime scene as quickly as possible had rankled badly. She hurried, and didn't believe she had compromised the investigation by doing so, but she wanted to be able to quote back chapter and verse of the Code if she ever again found herself in a similar situation.

Somehow, she didn't think the managers would have been so bossy if the inspector-in-charge had been one of the guys— Paavo Smith or Luis Calderon, in particular. Nobody told either of them what to do. Then there was Bo Benson, who would have worked out a give-and-take deal, or "Yosh" Yoshiwara, who would have found a way to get what he wanted and had the managers think it was their idea. Bill Sutter would have been a no-show. Only *she* could be pushed around. It was because she was a woman, she was sure—the only female homicide inspector in San Francisco.

She'd often been told that she was tough enough for the job. Well, boys, she was about to get even tougher.

Citing the Penal Code was one way to do it.

She sat scouring the complicated index at the empty secretary's desk when a guy she'd never seen before swaggered in. He was an inch or two shy of six feet, a hundred ninety or so pounds, and probably in his late thirties or very early forties. His hair was jet black, a little long and wavy on top, and his brown eyes heavy-lidded, down-turned and intense.

She pegged him right away. He was actually fairly good-looking, and could have been appealing, except for one thing. It wasn't the designer threads, the way he carried himself as if he had no fear, or the expensive hardware like the watch that probably cost half her yearly salary. It was those eyes—dark with a certain knowledge and experience—that told her which side of the law this smooth operator walked on. Her instincts twitched and her back stiffened.

"Hey, there," he said. His hands were in his pockets, and he looked over his shoulder a couple of times. "How you doing?" His voice was as mellow and buttery as soft, well-tanned leather.

"Okay," she said in an even tone. His wasn't the usual greeting for someone coming to this department. "This is Homicide," she pointed out.

"Yeah, I know." He glanced over his shoulder again. "I'm looking for someone. Paavo Smith."

She wondered if it was about a case. The guy looked nervous enough to be about to confess to murder. "Inspector Smith isn't in today. Perhaps I can help you."

He cocked an eyebrow, his gaze definitely rakish. "I'm sure you can, but not in this. I need a cop. What, is he off today or just out on a case? Can you reach him?"

What an a-hole. She stood up to her full five-foot ten-inch height and looked him straight in the eye. "I'm a homicide inspector," she said coolly. "Now, what is it you want, *sir?*"

He took a step back, hands raised as if to fend off a punch. "Whoa, I didn't know death cops came like"—he waved a hand toward her then quickly dropped it—"uh, yeah. Sorry. I just need a little info but, as you said, Paavo's not in today." He stopped; hard eyes studied her, then a half-smile, half-smirk curled his mouth. "Come to think of it, you probably can help. Why not, right?"

"Right." With cool detachment, she returned the look of scrutiny with one of her own and left him in no doubt that she not only found him wanting, but pictured him in an orange coverall. "Follow me."

She headed into the bureau. "With pleasure," he murmured, his voice deep, smooth and definitely sexy. Too bad his personality didn't match it.

If cops looked like her when he was growing up, he might have been more inclined to like them, Richie thought as he followed the attractive woman into a big, messy room. Rows of desks were hard to see because of all the paperwork piled up around them on bookcases, file cabinets, and computers.

"You read all this stuff?" he asked as she stopped at a desk and motioned him into a folding aluminum chair.

"No. I use it to cut paper dolls." Her chair tilted, swiveled and rolled. She leaned back in it comfortably.

He found himself grinning. So, she had a mouth that went along with the face and body. Not that she was his type. Far from it. To begin with, she was a cop. As they say on TV—*fuhgetaboutit.* And then, she was too tall. If she put on sky-high heels, they'd be like Mutt and Jeff. And he liked women who were soft in all the right places. She didn't look the least bit soft anywhere ... although, she had a body that wouldn't stop. The kind a man could get his hands around, so to speak.

She was older than he thought when he first walked in and saw her with one side of her straight blond hair tucked behind an ear, the other side draped down half covering her face as she poured over some thick books. When she looked up at him, her light touch with make-up added to the youthfulness. Her face was shaped like a triangle with widely set smoky-blue eyes and prominent cheekbones tapering down to a small, pointed chin. Most women he knew would give their eyeteeth for a bone structure and big eyes like hers. He was surprised she didn't doll up a little more—her white blouse, black slacks, and black boots with low one-inch heels looked like a uniform. But then he reminded himself that she was a death cop. Why bother to wow the corpses, right?

Although he felt a lot more alive now, just looking at her, than he had all morning.

She opened a spiral notebook. "Name?" she asked, reaching for the green pen at the corner of the desk.

He gripped the cold metal arms of the chair and shifted, trying to find a comfortable way to sit in the hard seat. "Richard Amalfi."

"Amalfi?" She stilled, a sudden question in her blue eyes. "You're related to Paavo's fiancée?"

"Yeah. Angie's a cousin."

"I see." She shut the notebook. Angie Amalfi was the bane of Rebecca's life. She had a serious crush on fellow homicide inspector Paavo Smith, but once he met Angie, he no longer even *saw* any other woman—not even if she sat at a nearby desk. "What can I do for you, Mr. Amalfi?"

"You can call me Richie,"—he glanced at the nameplate on her desk—"Rebecca."

"You can call me Inspector Mayfield." She twisted the top back onto the pen.

"Yes, ma'am, Inspector Mayfield, ma'am."

She regarded him like a schoolteacher with a truant.

His voice rumbled over the quiet room. "Look, I need you to help me find some, uh, friends. They're older ... gentlemen." He wracked his brain, trying to figure out how to best explain this. "They're in a van. Here's the license number." He pulled a piece of paper from his pocket and gave it to her.

"You want me to find this van?" she asked.

"Well ... yeah," he replied, palms upturned, open. "Why else would I be here? Call somebody and then tell me where it is. I got to go pick up the guys. They shouldn't be driving around this city all alone. It's a dangerous place, you know."

Her eyes narrowed. "How long has the van been missing?"

He slid back his sleeve and looked at his watch. "Nearly three goddamn hours." He ran his knuckles against his jaw as thoughts struck of what the guys could have done in that time.

"Three hours? That's not very long." She slid the paper with the license number to the corner of her desk. "I'm sure they'll turn up. They're probably sight-seeing or something."

"I called everybody I know." His loud voice echoed through the empty office. "Nobody said nothing about them showing up. This morning, I picked them up at the airport, and I'm supposed to see that they get someplace special this evening. That's all. But now, they're gone. And today's important."

"Because it's Christmas Eve?"

That's as good a reason as any. "Yeah, right. And it's up to me," he exclaimed, hands pressed to his chest, "to get them there." *Enough of this!* His impatience was about to boil over. He lowered his voice. "Look, Inspector, it's twelve old guys in a big Econoline." He leaned over her desk, picked up the license number and slapped it in front of her. "Call around. Maybe somebody's seen them."

She tapped the paper against the desktop. "Nobody's going to notice such a thing."

"They might."

"Why should they?"

He clamped his mouth tight. He really hadn't wanted to say, but she was right. There was no reason anyone would notice just any twelve old geezers. That wasn't the case here, though. He supposed he was going to have to tell her, much as he didn't want to. He would have told Paavo, but he trusted Paavo. Paavo was a man; he understood stuff. He didn't know if this skirt would. She acted kind of uptight, come to think of it. "Maybe I can reach Paavo at Angie's," he said, standing.

"And how is he going to help you?" She kept folding and unfolding the license number and seemed almost amused by his predicament. He was getting more pissed off by the second. She added, "Paavo's off duty."

He sat again. She was right, damn it. He looked back over his shoulder—an old habit, and one that gave him time to think. "Just a few phone calls to some dispatchers or something," he said. "Just to ask them if they've seen the van. That's all I need, and I'll take it from there."

She seemed to think for a minute, then nodded. He figured she wasn't exactly rolling in cases. "Okay. If that's what you want. I can make a few calls, but you're just wasting your time and mine. Nobody's going to have noticed."

"Well ... there's more to it," he admitted.

She waited.

He swallowed. "The twelve old guys I mentioned"—she nodded—"they're all dressed up like Santa Claus."

2

I F ANYONE HAD TOLD Rebecca Mayfield this morning that she'd end up in a black Porsche sitting next to a guy who looked and sounded like he stepped out of a bad remake of *Pulp Fiction,* she would have told him he was nuts. If he went on to say that she'd be investigating a Santa Claus corpse who looked flat as a mosquito on a car windshield and was now in hot pursuit of a van with twelve more jolly ol' Saint Nicholases, she'd have called the men in white coats for him.

She glanced at Richie Amalfi, who had just swung to the wrong side of the street to pass a cable car, nearly causing a head-on with a Gallo Wine truck, and suppressed the urge to stomp on the brake pedal—with his foot on it—and write him up.

Earlier, she phoned the dispatcher at Central Station and learned, to her amazement, that a report had come in from Chinatown about a van filled with Santa Clauses blocking the area around Waverly Place and causing a commotion. Waverly was a narrow side street parallel to Grant Avenue in the heart of Chinatown, and lined with tongs—legitimate family associations, or so they told the police. The dispatcher had just sent two squad cars to get the old guys out of there before the scene erupted into another tong war.

"Sounds like your boys are in Chinatown," Rebecca said to Richie when she got off the phone.

"Holy Christ!" Richie got up and headed for the door. "Thanks."

Mrs. Mayfield hadn't raised a stupid daughter. Some guy dressed in red pajamas had gone splat on her watch, and now twelve more were careening through the city with Lucky Luciano, here, in hot pursuit. There had to be some connection. No way would she believe it was a coincidence.

"Wait up!" She grabbed her purse, jacket, and was clipping her hair into a barrette at the nape of her neck as she followed him. "I'm going with you."

"No, you aren't." He spun on his heel in the doorway, hand on the frame as if to physically block her way.

"Yes, I am," she said, nose to nose with him as she put on the jacket. "You don't know where in Chinatown they are."

"It's a huge van. How hard will it be to find it?"

Her jaw jutted as she smiled. "You'll never know, will you?"

His eyes narrowed. "Why do you want to get involved in this?"

"Civic duty?" she suggested. "Helping the elderly? I mean *you*, not the Santa boys."

"Me?" He grinned and dropped his arm. "All right, Inspector. Have it your way."

They had another argument when they reached the parking lot. She didn't like getting into cars with strangers, although him being Angie's cousin helped. He absolutely refused to ride in her aging Ford Explorer and leave his car in the lot. Her choice was either to ride in the Porsche or to follow it—and then have to deal with parking, losing him in traffic, or having him simply take off and the Explorer be unable to keep up.

No argument. She folded her long body into the sleek little sports car, and was filled with suspicion over where and how he'd gotten it. The powerful motor hummed and darted into traffic.

"So," she said, assessing the cable-car passing, wine-truck menacing maniac at the wheel, "you picked up twelve old guys at the airport. Are they all friends?"

He sped up at the yellow light, hit the intersection as it turned red and cruised across. "Something like that, yeah."

After she peeled her fingers off the dashboard, she said, "You're obviously worried about them. They might get lost, I suppose."

"They know the city."

"No need to worry, then," she offered, closely watching his reaction.

His mouth wrinkled, but he didn't answer.

"What about their families?" she pressed. "Have you notified them?"

"Look, Inspector, cut the third degree. They're missing, all right? It's Christmas Eve. There are people they want to be with. Although"—brown eyes darted her way—"maybe you don't know about that kind of stuff. Why are you working today?"

She never answered personal questions from suspects. Not that he was one. Yet. "Tell me what you were doing with the old guys. It might help us find them."

"No family here, huh?" he persisted.

"My family's in Idaho, thank you. Now, if you expect me to help you, I need some information."

"They're going to ring bells for the Salvation Army." At her sneer, he added, "I volunteered to drop them off at their pot-stands."

An eyebrow lifted. "So you're one of Santa's little helpers."

"Well ..." He screeched to a halt behind a car that had stopped for a pedestrian. "Just like you said. Civic duty." He lowered the window, stuck his head out and yelled, "Move it, douchebag!"

Okay, she told herself, *so he's not going to tell me what he's up to.* She hadn't exactly expected he would. His furtiveness told her that it was probably shady and likely to end up with someone dead. Someone like her victim this morning.

She directed him toward Waverly Place. Half a block before reaching it, the traffic stopped completely. A crowd of people surrounded the entrance to Waverly.

Richie threw the car into reverse and was just about to careen backwards when another car pulled up behind him. And right behind it was a Coca-Cola truck. "What the—!" He pounded the steering wheel.

The streets of Chinatown were narrow, often one-way, and cluttered with double-parked cars and trucks unloading food, souvenirs, and tourists. The streets around Waverly were clogged under normal circumstances, and Waverly itself was even worse. Richie couldn't go backwards, forwards, or even along the sidewalk.

He shut off the motor, yanked out his key, jumped from the car and ran toward Waverly.

"Hey!" Rebecca climbed out and watched his retreating figure. What the hell, she thought, and took off after him. If someone stole or towed the Porsche, it was his problem, not hers. She mentally ticked off his fifth traffic violation in as many minutes: illegal parking.

Richie marched up and down the small street, puffing and snorting. "I don't see any van," he yelled. "Why don't I see the van?" He furiously kicked a bag of refuse, knocking it over. Its loose ties fell off, and rotting contents spewed onto the sidewalk. She eyed it, then him in distaste. Public littering.

"The report," she began, "said they went into a mahjongg parlor next to the Hop Sing Tong—"

Before she finished, Richie took off down the block. "There it is." He pointed toward a dark brown brick doorway. It was non-descript except for some Chinese writing painted on the side. She eyed it skeptically. "Don't tell me you read Chinese."

"No. Just the words"—he pointed at two characters—"mah and jongg."

With a calm swagger, Richie went inside. She'd never been in one of the Chinese gaming parlors before. They were illegal as hell, but the cops were under strict orders from the city fathers to leave them alone. You could either chalk it up to "understanding diversity" or "bribes." Take your pick. She followed.

The room was shrouded in a thick haze of smoke. Considering all the gambling taking place there, the city's "no-smoking in doors in any public places" policy was a non-factor. A jumble of tables with fluorescent lights over them filled the room. People sat, four to a table, looking almost like a bunch of bridge players except for the intensity of their expressions. Even now, in the afternoon, the room was nearly full. The clinking of game tiles was deafening. No one paid attention to the newcomers.

Richie strolled up to a pudgy bald-headed Chinese man at the desk and the two greeted each other like long lost pals. They talked quietly a while before the man shook his head and pointed up the street.

"They split," Richie said, not quite touching her as he ushered her toward the door. "He thought they were going to a restaurant, or trying to shake the cops who were looking for them, although, uh, they'd have no reason to be wary of cops," he quickly added. "None at all."

Her eyes narrowed with suspicion. "Why would they worry about cops looking for them in the first place?" she asked, although she already knew better than to expect an answer. She gave the players at the mahjongg tables one last *I'd-love-to-arrest-them-all-for-illegal-gambling* look, then let him steer her outside.

They reached the street just in time to see a large white van go by on the opposite end of Waverly Place, over on Washington Street. The van must have been double-parked or have done something people didn't like because a crowd of elderly Chinese men shook their fists and yelled after it in Cantonese. No translation needed.

"God damn!" Richie ran to Washington and watched the van lurch uphill. So did he. Rebecca sprinted up the hill with relative ease, and was surprised that he managed to stay in front of her.

The van turned at the corner onto Stockton, and by the time they reached the intersection, it was nowhere in sight. Richie bent over, hands on knees, trying to catch his breath, his face a brilliant shade of purple.

They returned to his car to find that the crowd had dispersed and his Porsche was now the only thing blocking traffic. The Coca-Cola and Toyota drivers stuck behind him had apparently decided to push it out of the way. One man tried to break into the car with a slim jim lockout tool while the other stood at the back of it, ready to push. Richie lifted the guy away from the car window, grabbed the lapels of his jacket, and tossed him onto the street.

The man looked up at the outraged Richie, apparently decided he had no complaints, and scrambled back to his beat-up Camry. The Coca-Cola driver followed.

Rebecca scowled at all three. Assault and battery on Richie's part, and possibly destruction of property depending on what happened to the Porsche once the two geniuses got it rolling since they were on a fairly steep hill. She was tempted to arrest them all, then go back to Homicide and use a more traditional approach to crime solving.

"You coming?" Richie asked as he got in. She hesitated, but Richie might be her only lead to the dead Santa for a long while. She jumped into the passenger seat and before she'd even shut the door, he stomped on the gas pedal.

"Why did the Santas go to the mahjongg parlor?" she asked and fastened her seat belt.

"Is that a joke?" He zigzagged past obstructions to proceed around the block. "Like, why did the chicken cross the road?"

"Ho, ho, ho." Her fingers itched to smack him. Hard. "What did they want in there?"

"They went for old time's sake, I guess," was his unsatisfactory response. For a man who emoted big time, he was remarkably tight-lipped, which meant he had secrets. She didn't like secrets.

The Porsche disappeared into the Stockton Street tunnel, the easiest route between Chinatown and the downtown area, and popped out near Union Square.

As opposed to Chinatown, which always resembled Hong Kong in the 1970's or '80's no matter what the season, holiday or time of year, the Square was lit with Christmas decorations. Up ahead was Macy's, to the right Saks Fifth Avenue. On the opposite street, the St. Francis Hotel, one of the city's oldest and finest, took up the entire block. Smaller exclusive shops and boutiques ringed the Square and nearby Maiden Lane. Rebecca couldn't afford a handkerchief in one of the Lane's shops, as opposed to Angie Amalfi and—by the looks of him—her insane cousin.

Here, people rushed about doing last minute Christmas shopping. She had gotten all hers finished two weeks before Thanksgiving. That was when stores held truly big sales, and there were no crowds. She could shop quickly, efficiently, and save money besides—not that she had many gifts to buy. But that wasn't the point.

Her Christmas season was efficient. No hubbub; no crowds teeming with energy. None of this kind of holiday excitement filling the air and making her spine tingle.

"Damn! Look at all these people." Richie broke into her thoughts as he waited impatiently three cars back from a red light. "I still have four presents to get. Looks like I'll be short."

"The disadvantages of your profession, I suppose." Her tone was thick with sarcasm.

Something flashed across his dark eyes. "My profession? You don't know beans about my profession. Maybe you should look at your own."

"What is your profession?" she asked.

He shrugged. "A little of this, a little of that."

"What did I tell you?" she said with a frown.

Just then, a laughing, package-laden couple jaywalked in front of them. He looked suddenly rueful and surprised her by saying, "Not exactly normal jobs for normal people, are they?"

Maybe it was the holiday bustle, maybe it was the sudden glint of honesty she saw on his face, or perhaps it was simply because they were both alone and working on Christmas Eve, but she said quietly, "Then we wouldn't be who we are, right?"

"Right." His elbow rested on the doorframe, hand to chin, and speaking more to himself than her in a voice so soft his words were almost imperceptible said, "Sometimes I wonder how bad that would be."

She glanced at him, but made no response. He met her gaze. The dark, almost hard-edge look she had found so off-putting when she first saw him seemed to have softened, or maybe it was because she was able to look past the surface coldness and found something deeper, more sensitive, even perhaps a little likeable.

The Porsche suddenly seemed a lot smaller, and he seemed a lot closer. The moment lengthened, but then she turned her head, facing straight ahead. From the corner of her eye, she noticed that he did the same. They sat in awkward, mutual silence, spectators to a festive, holiday scene; outsiders together.

The mood was broken when Rebecca spotted a large white van turning into the underground parking garage beneath Union Square. "Is that it?" she asked.

"We've got them now!" Richie punched the air as he swerved out of his lane, crossed oncoming traffic and zipped in front of cars lined up waiting to enter the garage. As he stopped to take his ticket from a parking garage machine, the burly driver he had cut off honked long and loud, then got out of his car and stomped toward them. Rebecca rolled down the window and held up her police badge. He backed off.

Richie roared up and down narrow parking lanes until he spotted the van. But it was already empty.

Nearby it, every parking space, nook and cranny was filled, often illegally, and he had to park an entire floor away. "Let's stay close to the lot." He headed for the elevator. "They should come back soon. You married?"

The question surprised her. "No," she replied, and focused back on the problem at hand. "Why not just wait near the van?"

"Hell, no." Thick concrete pillars held up the ceiling. Above was a park with trees, grass, and winter plantings. "I'll wait 'til I'm dead to have dirt and people walking around on top of me. Besides, I don't do underground in earthquake country. Engaged?"

"No." Not that it was any business of his, she thought. He was like a bulldog. "Don't you know the chance of there being an earthquake while we're waiting down here is practically zero?"

The elevator bell bonged and the doors opened. "Yeah? Tell that to the people who died going across the Bay Bridge during the last big one. I'm going up to the Square. I'll take my chances above ground."

"But you could be trapped in an elevator," she reasoned, stepping on.

"It's faster than taking the stairs." His hands twitched, his whole body bounced with nervous energy.

"What about tall buildings?" She wasn't sure if she was intrigued or simply enjoyed making him squirm. "Do you go up in them?"

"I would, if I had business up in one." When the elevator doors opened, he catapulted off it then tugged at his jacket in a show of casual indifference. It didn't fool her. "Let's walk around the park." He forged ahead without waiting, obviously ill at ease with her questions. Behind his back, she smiled.

The area was crawling with Santa Clauses. Everywhere they looked one or two stood, collecting money or handing out fliers. A violinist played *"I'm Dreaming of a White Christmas."* Rebecca usually could take or leave the song, but for some reason—perhaps because she was so alone this year—the song reminded her of Christmases past, when she was a child in Idaho, when her father was still alive and she was surrounded by family, and all of them enjoyed the snow-covered beauty of the land.

Her eyes grew misty. She felt Richie's gaze on her and tried to hide her feelings. She didn't like it that this man, practically a stranger, seemed to read her so well. The only man she'd met in a long time that she truly wanted to understand her was engaged to another woman, and probably spending a warm and joyous Christmas Eve with his fiancée.

How ironic was it that she was with that fiancée's scoundrel of a cousin?

They were soon out of range of the violinist, and neared a children's choir singing about city sidewalks dressed in holiday style. Suddenly, she found herself glad to be out of Homicide and here, surrounded by the warmth of the holiday—even if she was with a whack job a few trucks short of a convoy and searching for old coots who sounded like Santa's elves on speed.

"There they are!" Richie grabbed her hand and pointed toward the big, main entrance to Macy's a block away. "Come on!"

He plunged into the street, pulling her with him, jaywalking between cars and busses. She was glad the traffic was all but stopped due to the crowds. She couldn't believe he'd spotted the Santas. She could scarcely make them out in the chaos, and she'd been trained in crowd surveillance.

He ran up to them, approaching from behind them. "Wait!" he yelled, as soon as he was close enough for them to hear.

The Santas turned to face him. Each carried a Salvation Army kettle.

"Are you kidding me?" Richie's face went through a series of contortions: anger, disbelief, mulishness. He reached out and tugged at one of the Santa's beards. The elastic stretched and revealed a frowning but youthful mouth. "Uh ... sorry." Richie let go and the beard snapped back into place.

One Santa, bigger and more muscular than the others, stepped up to Richie, then shoved his donation kettle in Richie's stomach. Richie dropped a ten dollar bill in it, and then hurried away.

"It was a good try," Rebecca said.

"Yeah." He smoothed his shirt then the jacket, and ran his palm, diamond-pinky ring flashing, against the sides of his hair to smooth it. The whole time his back was to the Salvation Army Santas as if he couldn't care less about them.

They walked down to Market Street, heads swiveling from side to side, up and down a time or two. The streets swarmed with jaunty red caps and white beards mixed among the throngs of shoppers. "I've never seen so many goddamned Santa Clauses in my goddamned life!" Richie exclaimed.

Rebecca spotted a group of Santa hats marching toward the Ferry Building. "Are your Santas short?" she asked.

"Yeah! Where?" He looked where she pointed, then frowned. "What the hell. It's worth a try."

They hurried after the group, but slowed down as they neared. The Santas all carried boxes of Girl Scout cookies.

Richie kicked a mailbox, leaving a smudge from the sole of his shoe on it, and uttered a string of Italian curses. She ignored him, except to tick another violation: mutilating Federal property.

"This is dumb," he complained. "Let's get back to the van and wait."

"Why don't you tell me why you want to find the Santas?" she asked.

"Why don't you tell me why you care?" He shot back.

"Hey, you asked for help." She sidestepped the question.

"And aren't you supposed to be investigating murders?" he asked. "Nobody's dead. Just some old guys missing, yet you've glommed onto me like Crazy Glue. It doesn't fit, Inspector."

She wasn't ready to tell him about her dead Santa. Not with the way he'd been behaving.

They were in the parking elevator before she said, "Tell me why you need to find the Santas, and I'll tell you why I'm interested."

His eyebrows rose. "So you're saying you'll show me yours if I show you mine?"

"Fat chance!" she said with a glare.

He smirked—a smirk that quickly vanished when they got off the elevator.

The van was gone.

3

W HERE TO NOW, BOYS?" Joe Zumbaglio, otherwise known as Joey Zoom, asked as he slowly drove the van up and down the city streets. Skinny, with sagging cheeks and gnarled hands, he was seventy-five and the only one who still had a valid California driver's license—sort of. In case they got stopped, they didn't want to take any chances. The driver's license gave his name as Hiram Bernstein.

"I think we should'a stayed downtown." Lorenzo the Slug scratched his fake beard. He used to be called the Slug because he was so good with his fists—a slugger. Now, though, it was because he had to stop at a bathroom every thirty minutes so it took him forever, slug-like, to get from one place to another. That was also why the others let him ride shotgun next to Joey Zoom. He could get in and out of the van easily and no one had to sit next to him if they didn't find a john in time. Nobody told Lorenzo that, but let him think he was the same strong pugilist as ever. That was the thing about the crazy names the guys gave each other, they were for fun, honor, and at times, a surprising amount of affection.

"Three women handed me money," Lorenzo continued, his

brows thick with tangled white strands. "I was just standin' there, too. Wish I'da known how easy it was to make a buck wearin' a Santa suit. Woulda saved me a lotta trouble."

"What? You gotta pot 'a rubble?" Frankie Vines shouted. "What you gonna do wit' rubble?" Frankie didn't have a nickname. They tried to call him Frankie the Ear because of his obvious difficulties, but he thought they said Frankie the Beer and went on a toot that lasted three years.

As usual, everyone ignored him.

"How was we supposed to know everything's changed so much?" Lorenzo asked. "Who woulda thought Big Leo retired? I was countin' on him to help!"

"I told you I heard he died," Peewee Carducci whined in a high voice. He had a long narrow face and oversized ears that jutted out like wings under his Santa hat.

"Naw, Big Leo didn't die," Lorenzo said confidently, his scrawny Santa suit-clad chest puffed out. "We'll find him and get him to help. He knows everything, and if he don't wanna help, we'll make sure he remembers who he's dealing with."

"He don't remember nothing if he's dead," Peewee muttered.

"Who's Fred?" Frankie, formerly "the Ear," shouted.

"Maybe he's got alkaselzer," Guido Cucumber piped up. He was called that because of his love for antipasti, but he liked to brag that it was for another reason. Guido was round with a big belly, a jowly face and thick ankles that seemed to ooze over his shoes. "You know, that memory thing. Like Ronald Reagan had."

"Yeah, and maybe he thinks he's president, too," Joey Zoom remarked with a sneer. "Time's wasting. We gotta find him and take care of business. After that, maybe we should call Richie. Who's got his number?"

All were silent, but then two of the Santas were asleep, four had turned off their hearing aids, and two were too busy looking out the window to pay any attention to the conversation.

"Well, somebody's gotta have it," Joey Zoom muttered.

"At least we got ridda him," the Cucumber said, tugging on the Santa suit around his thick thighs where the material was cutting into his circulation. "And Joey Zoom still has his stuff." He high-fived the Santa next to him so hard that poor old Joey Aces, former card shark, fell off the seat. Six of the Santas were named Joe, which made things confusing sometime.

"Try North Beach," Lorenzo the Slug said. "That's where all the *paisans* hang out. And I gotta use a bathroom. Somebody there'll know how to find Big Leo." Everyone agreed.

As they drove by St. Francis of Assisi, they saw an elderly woman dressed in black step out of the church. She appeared confused, as if she wasn't sure which way to go.

Joey Zoom slowed way down, concerned about her, when two young men walked by. One of them grabbed her purse. She hung on tight and fell to the ground, but he yanked it hard and ran off with his buddy.

The van roared to life. Joey bore down on the thieves.

The young men angled right and so did the van. Pedestrians jumped out of the way; city trash bins flew. The guys turned down a narrow side street only to discover it dead-ended. High-pitched girly screams mixed with the squeal of brakes. The van stopped just in time. Six more inches and the assailants would have been spending Christmas in purgatory ... or worse.

Lorenzo jumped out, snatched the purse from the dumb-founded muggers who gawked in disbelief at the van of ancient Santas.

"Don't mess with little old ladies," Lorenzo yelled from the passenger seat as Joey Zoom backed the van out of the alley. "Or, with Santa Claus!"

4

———————

AS RICHIE DROVE in circles, speeding, swerving and swearing, around the downtown and Mission Street areas, Rebecca wondered once more if her guess that her dead Santa was connected to the missing Santas wasn't a bad mistake. Maybe she had had a sudden glucose attack from her failure to get a Snickers earlier that day. Maybe she'd let the lure of figuring out just what Richie Amalfi was up to, seduce her. Not, of course, that she would ever want to be seduced by Richie Amalfi!

She glanced at his dark, dangerous looks. Definitely not her type at all...although, he did kind of remind her of a younger, taller Al Pacino. She drew in her breath.

But if, as he'd said, there really were twelve Santas out there, why? What were they planning? She'd seen enough of Richie Amalfi to believe that any plan he was involved in had nothing to do with holiday giving.

Holiday taking was a better possibility. And now, it was up to her to prevent it. Whatever "it" was. She needed a different approach. One to lull him.

"Do you spend Christmas with Angie and her family?" she asked casually.

His eyebrows jiggled with surprise before he said, "Naw. My mother cooks. We eat. Watch a little TV if we can find a game worth paying attention to. Tell old family stories. I'll take home a plate of food that'll see me through the next couple of days." His gaze slid her way. "You?"

"I'm on call over the next thirty-six hours. So, I'll spend the day tomorrow basically hoping nobody gets killed. I won't see my family until January."

"What's—"

His question was cut off by the ringing of her cell phone. It was Traffic, calling with an answer to her earlier query.

She listened, then hung up and studied Richie. It was time for answers. Her voice turned hard. "Who do you know at the Stonestown mall?"

His face registered confusion. "Nobody. Why are you asking about the mall?"

"There was an accident—an auto accident—near the airport this morning."

"Yeah?"

"You picked your friends up at the airport."

"So?" He waited, and when she said nothing he swung the car into a red zone and shut off the engine. She braced herself for another explosion of temper, ready to meet it head on. Instead, he shifted in his seat to face her, his voice low, and somehow even more deadly. "You think just because I lost some old guys I'm responsible for everything that goes wrong in this town?" He sounded almost indignant. "What's with you, lady? Why are you here anyway? You can get the hell out of this car and go back to Homicide. It's not as if I'd miss your help."

She weighed her options. It would be in the newspapers soon anyway, so it wasn't exactly a state secret. "All right," she said. "Today, at ten-thirty or so, a car went off an overpass by the airport. It landed upside down and was pretty much flattened. By the time the cops and paramedics got there, though, the driver's body was gone. An hour later, a man dressed in a Santa suit was found at the mall. He was dead. His injuries made it look as if he'd fallen from a great height."

"A Santa suit?" Richie seemed dumbfounded by the story, but at the same time, his eyes darted. "What do you mean? Like he fell or jumped out of a building?"

"Maybe. The problem was, he was in the middle of the parking lot. There was nothing near he could have fallen from."

Richie blinked, and then slowly, a smile filled his face. "So ... it's sort of like he fell out of—"

"Yeah," she said quickly, not wanting to hear the words she knew he was thinking.

Richie chuckled.

"It's not funny!" Rebecca stated for the umpteenth time that day.

Something about her indignation made his chuckle develop into a belly laugh. "You're wrong, Inspector. It is funny. Maybe you should do blood work and give Santa a posthumous DUI." But when he glanced at her frown and his humor died. "Okay, so what does it have to do with me? You were at a mall, for cryin' out loud. They're lousy with Santas."

He was right—it should have made sense, but it didn't. "He wasn't wearing a mall-issued suit, for one thing. Wasn't recognized, had no I.D., and nobody seems to be missing any Santas but you. Are you sure you were expecting twelve Santas and not thirteen? Or maybe you only had eleven, and the dead guy is the twelfth?"

He looked startled at first, tense, then fell suspiciously quiet. "When I left the airport, I had twelve Santas," he replied, but then he asked, "What does he look like?"

"He's older, late sixties, seventies. Gray hair. A small guy. The photographer has probably e-mailed me copies of the best digital photos from the scene by now. If we go back to Homicide I can show you. Maybe you'll recognize him."

"I got a better idea." He reached behind the seat and pulled out an iPad mini. He turned it on, punched a few buttons, then held it toward her.

"Log onto your network," he said.

She shook her head. "Won't work. It's a closed, internal system, lots of security."

"Trust me."

Dubious, she took the device and did as told. In a matter of seconds, even faster than her supposedly secure terminal at work, she was into the system. She didn't want to think about it.

The photographer's photos were there. She flipped through them, then put the clearest one on the screen. "Are you squeamish about looking at dead bodies?" she asked.

"What, you think they'll give me nightmares or something?" Richie reached for the photo, glanced at it and blanched. Before he turned white then an anemic green, she saw recognition in his face. He handed the iPad back to her. "Never saw the guy before."

"You're lying."

"I never lie." He cranked the ignition and pointed at the computer. "Keep it close. Let's get going."

She put it in her handbag. "Where to?"

"I don't know. It's a small city, a big van. Something's got to show up."

"You're lying again! You've got someplace in mind." Any minute now, she was going to pull her Glock on him, no doubt about it. "Now, tell me where we're going."

Richie ran long fingers through blue-black hair that flopped in waves when he was through, almost but not quite thick enough to hide the small, thinning spot at the back of his head. She noticed a hint of gray at the temples, a slight cragginess to the skin, and lines at the outer corners of his eyes. Normally, she liked such signs of maturity in a man. She might need to rethink that.

Richie's next comment brought her back to earth. "I said I didn't recognize the guy in the photo. But I know someone who might."

The building was shaped like a triangle. The pointed nose, on the corner of Columbus Avenue, held the front door. In the early days of the last century, LaRocca's Corner was one of the most popular mob hangouts. These days, it was mostly filled with yuppies who liked its post-Prohibition décor and its wise guy wannabe customers. Rebecca never doubted, however, that a few of the real thing continued to frequent it as well.

Richie's mouth scrunched as he perused Rebecca head to toe. "I better go in alone. You wait."

She said firmly, "No."

"They'll wonder who you are. What you're doing with me."

"Tell them I'm a friend."

He tugged an earlobe, and looked uncomfortable. "Well ..."

She glanced down at her black jacket, slacks, boots, and white blouse buttoned to the collar. She'd pulled her hair back in a barrette as they'd left Homicide. He was right. She didn't look like someone a guy like him would hang around with. Which was, in her opinion, not a bad thing.

"Just wait a minute." She dug some lipstick out of her purse and put it on, then unfastened the barrette and shook her hair loose. Taking off the jacket, she removed her gun from her back-of-the-waist holster and put it in a zippered compartment in her

Galco holster handbag. Next she cinched her belt tight, and rolled the sleeves of her blouse to the elbows and unbuttoned the top two ... no, the top three ... buttons and spread the collar wide.

"Now?" She expected the scrunched-mouth look again. Instead, she noticed his Adam's apple move as if he swallowed hard as his gaze slowly drifted down her long frame, and then back up again. He reached up and gently pushed a couple of strands of hair back from her eye. To her surprise, his expression softened as he gazed at her. Then he nodded. For some reason, her pulse began to beat a bit faster at his touch.

They walked inside with his arm around her waist. He kept her close as they approached the bar, waving to people, calling out greetings in Italian and English, and using the kinds of nicknames she thought had been made up for shows like *The Sopranos*.

He ordered bourbon and water and quietly asked her what she wanted. She hesitated a fraction of a second then said, "Gin and tonic."

The understanding in his eyes was even more unsettling than the fact that she had ordered alcohol on duty. Well, she could order it, but it didn't mean she had to drink it.

As he talked to the bartender and others, she pretended to sip her drink, listening carefully, even though little of what they said made sense. Most of it was almost in code, and sounded suspiciously like the kinds of conversations one might have with a bookie. The only difference was that this time of year they talked football, not horses. Christmas and college bowl games seemed to go better than mistletoe and holly in this little establishment.

A very drunk man staggered over and put his arm around Richie. "How's it goin' pal?" he slurred.

"Fine, Pinky. Looks like you've got a heat on. You got cab fare to get home?"

"Naw. I'm not ready to go home anyway." He eyed Rebecca suspiciously. "Say, where's Sheila?"

"She's home with the kids. Let's get you a cab."

"No need, Richie, really."

Richie sweet-talked him to the door.

Home with the kids? Rebecca hadn't thought of Richie as being married. He didn't seem settled, and hadn't mentioned a wife and kids earlier when he talked about Christmas at his mother's. He might be divorced, but then, a lot of these "wise guy" types didn't talk about their wives. The women kept the house, raised the kids, and prayed in church for the ever-deteriorating souls of their husbands, but nothing more.

Given all she'd seen so far, it was interesting that Richie Amalfi was on Angie's father's side of the family. From what Paavo told her, Sal Amalfi was a straight arrow—a businessman who had made millions on shoe stores and real estate. Angie's mother's relatives were another story. One branch of Serefina's family, headed by her uncle Bruno Bacala, also called Bruno the Tweeds because of his stylish clothes, was connected up to the armpits.

Richie placed his hand on her arm, startling her out of her thoughts. She hadn't heard him return. "Have you got the gizmo in your purse with the picture of the dead body?"

She handed the iPad over and he showed the bartender.

"Sure I know him," the man said. "It's Cockeyed Lanigan. Mean old coot."

"He's dead," Richie stated.

"No fooling? Man, the old guys are dropping like flies. Nobody's going to mourn Lanigan, though, you can count on that."

"Any idea why he'd be headed to the airport this morning?"

"Not me. The only guy who ever talked much to him was Punk Leo. Maybe he knows."

Richie's attention was distracted from the bartender when a new customer came in laughing about some old Santas who broke up a mugging just outside St. Francis. The kids they caught not only gave up the old lady's purse, but went into the church to thank God they were still alive.

The clientele at LaRocca's Corner laughed as if it was the funniest thing they'd ever heard.

Richie was all over the newcomer finding out just where the van was, who was in it, and where it was going. The information didn't help much, but at least they knew the Santas were in the neighborhood.

By the time they left LaRocca's, the sun was setting. "Damn!" Richie said, scowling at the sky. "Soon, it's going to be harder than ever to find them." He checked his watch. "I've only got four hours."

"Then what?" Rebecca asked, putting her jacket back on, rebuttoning the top of her blouse, and capturing her long hair once more into a barrette. "Your Santas turn into a pumpkin?"

His mouth wrinkled into a worried frown. "No, but I might."

Just then, right before their wondering eyes did appear ... a big white Econoline filled with little old men. The van headed up Columbus Avenue, then turned onto Mason.

"Holy shit!" Richie cried and took off after it.

The van started up a hill. Richie and Rebecca tried to catch it but were losing ground when a cable car clanged for them to get out of the way. As it went by Rebecca grabbed the pillar that went from the back guardrail to the roof. She used it to pull herself onto the bottom step on the side of the cable car.

Richie was behind Rebecca and couldn't grab the same rail, but lunged for the back of the car and managed to grab the top of the guardrail. He had to run fast to keep his footing, and then he shot up, lifting a foot onto the bottom rail and pulling the second foot up after it. He held on tight.

"Rebecca! Watch out!" he suddenly shouted.

She had been looking at him, and now turned to see the back end of a UPS van jutting out into traffic, only a half-foot from the side of the cable car.

She stared at it, shocked, when he wrapped an arm around her shoulders and yanked her body hard against his, then held her close to the back of the cable car as they zipped past the UPS van with only inches to spare.

As she watched, she knew her face and every other part of her would be decorating the van right now if it weren't for Richie's quick thinking.

On the other hand, she wouldn't be in this predicament or on this cable car in the first place if it weren't for him! She wasn't sure if she should thank him or slug him.

She might decide after she stopped shaking.

He was still holding her tight when a red-faced conductor stormed out of the cabin. "What the hell is wrong with you two idiots? If you want to commit suicide you do it on somebody else's car! Now get inside and pay like everyone else, or get the hell off!"

The cable car was halfway to the next corner when it had to stop behind a row of cars for a red light. Richie saw that the van was stopped as well.

Ignoring the conductor, he leaped off the car and ran toward the van. When Rebecca saw what he was up to, she followed, but not before mouthing "Sorry," to the outraged ticket-taker.

Violation: riding public transportation without paying fare.

"Open up!" Richie yelled, tugging on the driver's locked door handle and pounding on the window. "What's the matter with you guys?"

Rebecca was on the passenger side, yanking on the doors,

but they were also locked. She looked inside, and sure enough, just as Richie had promised, rows of little old Santa Clauses sat, their dark brown eyes gaping back at her in surprise and wonder. She had to admit that until that very moment, a part of her simply hadn't wanted to believe his story was true.

She pulled on the door handle of the front passenger door with both hands, one foot on the frame for leverage, demanding the fellow inside open it, when the light turned green. Other cars began to move. Suddenly, the door swung open and slammed hard against her. The window hit her nose, hurtling her end over end. Black lights and bright stars exploded in her head. Luckily, she rolled in the direction of the sidewalk out of the way of the oncoming cars. The van rocketed away.

Richie's hands tucked under her armpits and lifted as he half-dragged her out of the street and over to the curb where they both sat. "You okay?" He took out a handkerchief—she didn't think anyone used them any more—and lightly pressed it to her nose. Maybe in his line of business he needed one. When he lifted it away, she saw blood. There was no maybe about it.

"Does it feel broken?" he asked.

The world turned as red as her blood. She'd been dragged all over town, had a drink in a bar with a nest of criminals, broke enough laws to spend a week in jail, nearly got wiped out while riding a cable car, and now she'd been hit in the nose by a van of Santas! Her breath started coming short and fast, her ears rang, and her entire world began to tilt.

Suddenly, he grabbed the back of her head, shoved it between her knees and held it down. Her hand found his chest and she shoved him away. He let go of her, and she sprang back up. "What the hell are you doing?" she shrieked.

"You turned white as a sheet! I thought you were going to pass out," he said. "You gotta take it easy. How does your nose feel?"

"Take it *easy*?" Her temples pounded. "How can I take it easy around you! You moron! You dolt! You—" She grabbed the handkerchief from him as she felt blood trickling down her nose to her upper lip and covered both. She gingerly felt her nose. It didn't feel broken, thank God! "You pithant!" She lisped.

"Calm down," he ordered as if talking to a child. "You're hurt."

"I'll show you hurt!" She swung her arm and socked him in the ear, hard, then jumped to her feet.

"Ow!" He rubbed the side of his head. "What did you do that for?"

"I must be crathier than you are to have wathted my time on you and your bullthit!" The thought that she was no closer to knowing why he was driving around with the Santas, what he was up to, how it was all connected to her dead guy, and the fact that she was lisping, turned her purple with rage.

A car driving by stopped and a middle-aged man gawked at her, his mouth hanging open. She stepped towards him. "What'th your problem?" she demanded. He sped away.

She spun back to Richie, still sitting on the curb watching her in stunned silence.

Abruptly, she stopped, stared down at him, then lifted her head and walked away, handkerchief still pressed firmly to nose.

He shook his head in wonder, then got up and followed.

5

———————

THE TWELVE SANTAS marched single file into LaRocca's Corner wishing Merry Christmas to one and all. Half of them followed Lorenzo the Slug in a rush to the bathroom, while the others took over two tables, three barstools, and ordered twelve Boiler Makers. Earlier, they'd had lunch at the replacement for the Old Spaghetti Factory, and espresso at the replacement for the Café Trieste. Neither, they'd concurred, was as good as the "real" places they remembered.

Once they got settled, after a few words with the bartender about the Good Ol' Days, Guido Cucumber said, "By the way, we're looking for Big Leo Respighi. Seems he's given up mahjongg. Even closed his business. What's up? You know where we can find him?"

The bartender looked surprised. "Leo? I hadn't heard he'd closed up shop. I suspect he's home with the old lady."

"No way," Guido said. "His wife's dead."

Stricken, the bartender put down the rag he'd been wiping glasses with. "Anna Maria?"

"Hell, no!" Guido scowled. "That's Punk Leo's wife—"

"Don't call him Punk if you know what's good for you," the bartender warned.

"Who cares?" Guido said. "We're talking his father—*Big* Leo."

"Hey, fellows, I'm sorry," the bartender said. "But *Big* Leo died about six, seven years ago."

The other Santas were listening and they all doffed their caps in memory of the now Dead Leo.

"See, I told you he was dead!" Peewee muttered.

"We gotta plan." Lorenzo the Slug sat at a table and the Santas gathered around him. "I thought Big Leo would be the one to help us. He knew a lotta things money can't buy. We needed him, and now he's dead. The rat!"

"Poor Dead Leo," Guido Cucumber muttered.

"I got an idea," Joe Pistolini, called Joe the Pistol for obvious reasons, said. "I know a woman who'll help us. Her uncle's a good friend."

"I hope so," the Cucumber said. "I'm starting to get a little tired with all this eating and drinking and gabbing. I gotta save my energy for tonight."

The others wearily concurred.

As Richie walked alongside Rebecca back to his Porsche's parking spot, he tried to figure out if he should ditch her somewhere. He had to admit, for some weird reason he liked having her there, but she had no part in this, and it could end up being dangerous for her.

Somebody was pulling a fast thone here, and he nwas in the middle of it. What if the extra Santa had shown up at the airport and said he was supposed to be part of the group? Richie wondered if he'd have believed him and let him join the others. Or even worse—what if he would have bumped off one of the real passengers and took his place? Would the others have known he didn't belong? In fact, what if one of them already *was* a fake? What if they'd all been kidnapped? How could he explain how he'd let *that* happen on his watch?

The thought turned him ashen.

Some insider had to have leaked out the information about the Santa costumes. Who was the snitch, and whose side was he on? Were the old boys, right now, in danger?

He doubted it. They hadn't looked the least bit scared when they sucker punched Rebecca with the van's door. The nerve of those guys picking on a woman that way ... unless they decided she was the one who posed the most danger to them.

He only hoped she didn't end up with two black eyes as a result. The lady, he had discovered, had a temper.

He had chuckled about the Santa costumes when they were first proposed. These old geezers were only "somebodies" in their own minds, he had thought. Some had served time. Others were lucky, had never been caught, and the statute of limitations had long passed on anything they might have done.

On the other hand, considering that they were now on the lam and another Santa was dead, maybe they'd been right to be paranoid.

He thought about letting someone on the inside know what was happening, but doing so meant he had to admit that he'd lost the twelve guys. Twelve! Who in the hell loses twelve men? That was more than a frigging football team!

It was embarrassing. Not to mention potentially deadly. Scratch the "potentially." Much as he hated to admit it, Rebecca Mayfield and her resources in the police department were his last, best hope at finding them.

The chance of the Santas being picked up by the cops was high. Frankly, he never imagined they could drive around in a van all day and not get nailed. None of them could drive a straight line, he was sure, and he doubted they could keep this up for very long now that it was dark out. Half the guys had cataracts and the other half were legally blind. No way could they continue night driving without running into something.

Once that happened, Rebecca would get the call from the dispatcher, and he'd rush with her to wherever they were, pick up the pieces and deliver them on time.

"Your nose stop bleeding?" he asked.

"Yes." She'd put the handkerchief in her purse. "I'll send the hankie back after I wash it."

"It's not important."

When they reached a street lamp, he stopped walking. "Wait," he said, then turned to her and put his hand under her chin, studying her face in the light. "I don't think you'll have a shiner for Christmas."

"Good! I don't want anything to remind me of this day!" She pushed his hand away.

He tried not to chuckle, but failed. He started walking again, and she continued at his side.

"It's not funny," she muttered.

The way she had lost her temper irritated her. Paavo Smith would never have done anything so undignified, and she shouldn't have either. She decided to put things back on an even keel.

After a while, she said, "Your kids must be excited about Christmas. Are any young enough to still believe in Santa Claus?"

He jumped. It wasn't the kind of question a guy liked to hear. "My *what*?"

"Kids. The ones you talked about at LaRocca's."

"I don't have any kids! None that I'll admit to, anyway," he added. An old joke. He was sure he didn't have any, though he'd lived pretty wild in his younger days.

He glanced at Rebecca. She was basically a quiet woman, but he liked it when she talked to him, even if she said some oddball stuff. "What made you think I had kids?"

She looked confused. "Somebody asked about Sheila, and you said your wife was home with the kids."

"Wife? No way! She's an old girlfriend. A widow. She's got kids. May her husband rest in peace, but after I dated her awhile, I could see why he decided to check out so young. I don't have anything to do with her anymore. Or ... not much."

"No wife, no girlfriend?" she asked.

"No wife. Lots of girlfriends," he said with a grin. "None serious. Not lately, anyway. You?"

She thought about Greg Horning at home in Cleveland for Christmas. "Could be," she admitted. "I'll see how it works out after the holidays."

He nodded. "Another cop?"

"Sure. Who else do most cops date but other cops?" she asked with a rueful shrug. "We're the only ones who understand us."

"That's what I figured," he said. "I warned my cousin Angie about that, but the Amalfis are all pretty stubborn."

Her eyebrows lifted. She couldn't imagine anyone having a negative thought about Paavo Smith. He was the best cop she'd ever met. Angie Amalfi, on the other hand ... "That's funny, because all of Homicide warned Paavo about Angie."

He did a double take. "Are you crazy? Angie's a great catch."

Rebecca frowned. "A lot of women go for the uniform."

"Paavo's plain clothes." Richie eyed her. "Why? Who do you think is better suited for him?"

She stared straight ahead. "I have no idea."

He eyed her firm mouth, her small pointed chin, jutting proudly. "Oh, yeah?" he asked. He wanted to smirk, but didn't dare.

She glared as if she'd gladly see him burst into flame. "That's what I said."

They reached his car and got in.

"Where to?" she asked.

"Telegraph Hill."

"Why?"

"I've got to talk to somebody."

In just a couple of minutes, he stopped in the driveway of a house half way up Telegraph Hill on Vallejo Street. "Wait here." He got out of his Porsche.

To his irritation, she got out of the car as well. Before he could object, she said coldly, "If you think I'm about to twiddle my thumbs in your car while I've got a dead body to investigate, you're wrong. If this guy knows anything, I'm going to hear it."

"He won't talk to a cop," he shouted, arms spread straight out at his sides and his face so close to hers they were almost nose-to-nose.

"He'll talk if I take him in!"

He straightened, doing a slow burn and running his hand along the back of his head. She was going to get him bloody well killed! He tried not to shout, to be reasonable, but it didn't work with her. "For what reason could you arrest him? Because I think he might know something? That won't work. He'll simply say I was wrong. Look, Inspector, I need to find my twelve guys. If they know something about your dead merry old elf, you'll find out, but only after I've got them. So, back off!"

"Go to hell," she said calmly.

"Trust me," he pleaded, running out of ideas and time.

"Not on your life! Who lives here?"

"It's Punk Leo's place. But you can't call him that to his face. Just Leo. Leo Respighi."

"I want to see him."

He glared. "Then keep your mouth shut and don't—whatever you do—let on that you're the law!"

She glared right back. "I'm not making any promises."

He clamped his jaws shut and grudgingly led the way up the outside stairs to the front doors. As they went, he noticed that she quickly removed the barrette and fluffed her hair a bit, and even smoothed and adjusted her blouse. Except for the bruise on her nose, a drop of blood on her blouse, and the smudge on her face, to him the lady looked damned fine.

There were three doors in the style common to San Francisco flats. He rang a bell and one of the doors buzzed open. Inside a narrow foyer they faced another long flight of stairs.

"Hey, *paisan*—it's me, Richie."

"Richie! *Caro mio!*" A woman's voice called down. As they reached a bend in the stairs, they looked up to see a middle-aged woman with a square face and short, black curly hair standing at the landing. She wore an apron and was wiping her hands, a diamond and platinum ring on nearly every finger, then held her arms out to give Richie a big hug. He hugged her in return.

She stepped back and eyed Rebecca. "Who's this? A new girlfriend, Richie? She's very pretty."

He took Rebecca's hand and pulled her forward. "This is, uh, Becky May ... Mason. Becky, meet Anna Maria Respighi." Anna Maria grabbed her hands and welcomed her. Richie was glad Anna Maria kept her mouth shut about Rebecca's nose. Probably because she'd seen a lot worse than that being married to Punk Leo.

"Is Leo here?" Richie asked.

"He's in the back, watching TV. I'll go get him. Sit down in the kitchen. You hungry, Richie?" She patted his face. "You and your girlfriend, you want to eat something?"

"No, sweetheart," he said. "We're fine. Just got to talk to Leo."

"*Aspetti.* You come to my house, you eat." She gave them both a glass of red wine and made up plates of leftover rigatoni and meatloaf still on the counter from dinner. While she zapped them in the microwave, she lit herself a cigarette and asked Richie in Italian all about his new girlfriend. He only prayed Rebecca didn't understand as he sang her praises in the bedroom and the kitchen—the only places he could think of that really mattered. He decided she didn't have a clue what he was saying since she neither blushed or shot him with the gun she was packing in that big black purse she lugged around everywhere. Come to think of it, she probably never blushed.

With the cigarette smoldering in an ashtray, Anna Maria put a plate in front of Richie, and another before Rebecca. "*Mangia,*" she said, then softly to Rebecca. "I hope you like it."

She said it so sweetly, Rebecca found herself murmuring, "I'm sure I will." The smell of the spicy red sauce and the hint of garlic, onion and oregano in the warming meatloaf, reminded her that she was starving. The food was delicious.

Richie, too, ate with gusto. "You're looking too skinny, Richie," Anna Maria said.

"I'm not skinny—just not so heavy anymore. I was letting myself go. The hell with that. I joined the gym. Run, box. It's good for me. I actually feel better."

"You were overweight?" Rebecca asked between bites.

"For a little while," he murmured, then stuck his head further down toward his plate.

"A woman," Anna Maria said in explanation to Rebecca as she stood by the open back door for the last few drags. "It's a long story."

"And not one I came here to talk about, Anna Maria," he said, washing down a swallow with wine. "So anyway, where's Leo?"

Rebecca found the previous conversation interesting, however. "Was that Sheila?" she asked Anna Maria.

"Sheila? No, no, no. It was Mary. She was—"

"Enough already!" Richie shouted.

Anna Maria smiled fondly at him, crushed the cigarette butt, patted him on the arm as if in consolation, and then headed down the hall to get her husband.

Rebecca's eyebrows were still high on her forehead, wondering what all that was about. "Seems like a lot of women in your life."

He shrugged.

She found herself strangely curious about him and was going to try to find out more when a big man walked into the kitchen wearing a satin robe patterned with Christmas trees and reindeer on a red background. Richie stopped eating and Rebecca nearly dropped her fork.

Punk Leo's bare legs looked like toothpicks below the robe, and his feet were shod in loose, floppy brown leather slippers. "'Ey, Richie, how's it going?" His deep voice reverberated throughout the kitchen like a boom box.

Leo sat down at the table. Richie introduced Leo and Rebecca, calling her his "acquaintance." Leo's brows slanted downward as he nodded. Leo's nose, lips and ears were all over-sized and blubbery. The only things small were his eyes and, it seemed, his intelligence.

"We're trying to find out who this guy is." Richie pretended not to know Cockeyed Lanigan as he showed Punk Leo the thirteenth Santa's photo on the small computer screen.

Leo no sooner looked at it then practically threw it back at Richie as he bellowed, "I don't know him, and I don't want to know him."

"What do you mean?"

"He's trouble. I don't have nothing to do with him. Nothing. Is that clear? I don't even want to hear his name in my house."

"He's dead, Leo," Richie said starkly.

Leo's face darkened. "Dead? You show a picture of a dead guy to me? You do that in my house! Bring me seven years bad luck! Are you crazy?" He lunged, toppling Richie and his chair to the floor.

Anna Maria started shrieking for them to stop.

Using his arms and legs, Richie was trying to shove the big man off him. Rebecca avoided where she looked as the two scrambled on the floor and the bathrobe lifted, revealing more of Leo than she'd ever wanted to see.

Rebecca made one attempt to pull Leo off Richie, who looked like he was in danger of being smothered, and got an elbow buried in the stomach for her troubles, doubling her over to gasp for air. The gun she had in her purse tempted her, but it would give away that she was a cop, and Richie had warned her not to. She could use some of the karate she'd learned, but she didn't like the idea of breaking anyone's bones on Christmas Eve.

Anna Maria solved the dilemma by grabbing a dust mop and shoving and shaking the head of it between the two men, bopping first Leo then Richie in the face. Clouds of dust billowed with each smack. When the men started coughing, she swung the mop even more forcefully, hitting their noses and foreheads, then chest and shoulders. With each swing, more dust flew, making them pant more, which meant they had to take bigger and bigger gulps of air and only managed to get even more dust in their mouths.

Finally, they let go of each other and rolled to their sides, eyes watering and choking.

Cold-cocked by a dust mop. Rebecca tried not to laugh, but as she looked from Punk Leo to Richie gasping from their exertions, she couldn't help herself. The thought struck that in some crazy way, despite everything, this madness around her was funny. Her gaze settled on Richie, and she realized she hadn't been around such a provocative but interesting man in a long, long time. God! Where had that thought come from? The crack on her nose must have been harder than she'd thought.

"Cover yourself, Leo!" Anna Maria yelled, still wielding her mop. "What's wrong with you two? It's Christmas Eve! You should be ashamed!"

As Anna Maria helped Leo struggle off the floor, Rebecca held out a hand to Richie.

"You get that filth out of my house!" Leo roared, facing Richie again. "I don't know Cockeyed Lanigan and I don't give a damn that he's dead!"

"Do you know what he was up to this morning?" Richie asked, stubborn as usual.

Leo went beefy red. "What are you, some kind of cop? I don't know nothing! Get the hell out of here, Richie," he said. "And if you know what's good for you, you'll go home and forget about all this."

"The cops will find out what happened, Leo. Homicide's on the case, and you know how stubborn, pig-headed, and worse than a dog with a bone, those people are," Richie said with a glance at Rebecca and wearing a lopsided grin. "After all, Cockeyed Lanigan's dead."

"Yeah?" Leo adjusted his robe. "Then that means there really is a Santa Claus."

6

THE SANTAS WERE STANDING outside the Fior d'Italia restaurant waiting to meet the woman Joe the Pistol had phoned. To their surprise, as they cheerfully wished Christmas greetings to passers-by, people kept handing them money.

They took it.

Then, a little boy and girl went walking by. The boy looked about seven and the girl six. They stopped, glared at the Santas and stuck out their tongues.

As they started to walk away, Guido Cucumber limped after them. "What's the matter with you kids?" he yelled. "Don't you know better than to treat Santa Claus that way?"

"We hate Santa," the boy said.

"Yeah, we hate you," the girl chimed, but her blue eyes filled with tears.

"Hey, what's wrong? Santa didn't do nothing to you," Guido protested.

"You aren't coming to our house," the boy said. "Daddy's sick and can't work. We wanted bikes, but Daddy said no way. Santa doesn't give things like that to poor kids. Seems to me, the rich kids could get their parents to pay for things, so it's the poor ones Santa should help."

The Cucumber nodded. "Well, your Daddy may be right most of the time, but there's twelve of us Santas here, and maybe we can work something out. You tell me where you live, so I won't have trouble finding the right house, and maybe between the twelve of us, we'll be able to help you."

The kids looked wary. "I thought Santa Claus knows where everybody lives," the boy said.

"Well, yeah, but look at us, we're getting old. You know old people are forgetful sometimes."

The kids gave their address, and all the Santas wished them Merry Christmas as they left.

"What are we gonna do?" one of the Joes asked.

"Think guys. Who do we know who can help?" Guido looked from one to the other.

"Santa's dead," Peewee said remorsefully. "We know all about it."

"Where's Santa's bed?" Frankie, formerly "the Ear," shouted. "I'm ready to lay down. All this is a lotta work!"

They ignored him, as usual.

"No problem. I know someone," Joe the Pistol said with a big smile. "Big Leo's kid, Punk Leo. He sells toys and all kinds of stuff. I'm going to his house tomorrow for Christmas dinner. We can call him."

Joey Zoom stared at him, annoyed. "Did you tell him we was all coming here today? We weren't supposed to tell no one."

"What's the big deal? He's expecting me," the Pistol argued. "His wife's aunt's husband was my wife's brother-in-law, God rest his soul, so we're related. I told Punk Leo not to worry, that we was all dressed in Santa costumes so nobody'd recognize us."

"I hope you're right," Guido Cucumber said, "and I hope he knows enough to keep his mouth shut."

"Sure he does. Let's go find a pay phone. I'll call him. You'll see. Punk Leo's a nice guy, despite what everybody says about him. He'll get some bikes and deliver them to those kids. No problem."

"Hey, wait a minute," Lorenzo the Slug said, his bushy eyebrows knitted with suspicion. He'd come in late to the conversation since he was using the snazzy facilities at Fior d'Italia. "If you talked to Punk Leo, how come you didn't know Big Leo's dead?"

Joe the Pistol shrugged. "I ain't talked to Big Leo since the summer of eighty-three. We had a fight. I was gonna ask Punk Leo about him when we got together. Don't need to now."

"What was the fight about?" Lorenzo asked.

Joe looked remorseful. "Damned if I can remember."

"You were talking about Stonestown," Richie said after a long silent period punctuated only by curses as more time elapsed without a van sighting. It was nearly seven-thirty. "I remember that Punk Leo runs an import-export business. Furniture, toys, all kinds of stuff. I'm pretty sure his warehouse is right by Stonestown."

Rebecca's head snapped toward him. "That means he probably ships furniture around the country, or the world. He would have access to large crates, easily big enough for a body."

"Exactly," Richie said.

The more Rebecca thought about it, the more sense it made. Wrap the body up good, pack it in a furniture crate, put on a sticker to Madagascar, and then pay a few bribes once it arrives. Who'd know? Or, even simpler, ship it to Las Vegas and pay some friends down there to create another lump out in the desert far from town. Easy. But, *why?*

And, if someone were trying to get Cockeyed Lanigan's body to Leo's shop, what if they freaked out at all the security around the mall due to Christmas, dumped the body and took off?

"Let's go check the place out," she said.

"I don't think so." Richie looked at her as if she'd lost her mind. "My guys won't be at Leo's business."

"How do you know?" she retorted. "He acted more than a little suspicious. He clearly knows more than he's saying."

There was more under-the-breath muttering about women and cops. "All right, Inspector. We'll take a quick look, then we're out of there and back to North Beach. I've got the feeling they aren't far away."

Stonestown was almost completely deserted since it closed early on Christmas Eve. They found Punk Leo's import-export business, then drove to the loading dock area in back of the building. All the lights were out. It looked quiet and empty.

Richie parked along the side of the building, then they tried the doors, hoping to find one open and something going on in the warehouse. They didn't.

"Well, it was worth a try," Richie said, dejected. "I should give this up. I don't know where else to look, what else to do. I guess it's time for me to face the music."

"Which means what? Are you in trouble? We've spent the whole day searching, Richie, and I don't even know why."

For a moment, the way he gazed at her, she thought he might open up. He didn't. "You don't want to know. Trust me. I'm supposed to deliver them somewhere. That's all there is to it."

They started to walk back to his car. "Well, maybe they'll go there on their own," she consoled.

"They don't know where it is. It's a secret." He glanced over his shoulder a moment. "I'm sure they expect someone will help them, but I can't if I don't know where they are."

"That makes no sense," she insisted.

"It doesn't, except that they're old guys who are used to others looking out for them."

"As in, they've been in jail most of their lives?" Rebecca asked suspiciously.

"As in ... you might be right about that. Whatever it means, I lost them, and I'll have to pay the consequences."

"You make it sound as if the consequences are dangerous." They parted and he walked toward the driver's side, she to the passenger's.

He looked upward. The stars shone brightly in the clear night sky, the moon just rising over the mountains. "I'll find out," he said.

He was maddening. It was like talking to a cipher. "Well, you might be wise to worry." She faced him over the top of the car. "A killer is out there somewhere. Maybe he's hunting down your Santas—maybe not. But he's there, and if you're involved, you could be in danger as well."

"Me? I never do anything dangerous. I'm allergic to it."

Just then a shot rang out. Richie ducked after feeling the bullet whistle by his head. Rebecca dropped behind the Porsche. A dumpster was behind her and she ran to it, curled between the trash bin and the wall, waving for Richie to follow. He did.

As far as she knew, Richie Amalfi wasn't armed. But she was. She slid the gun from the special pocket in her handbag. She thumbed the safety off and waited. One more shot, and she'd see where the shooter was hiding.

"Cover me," he whispered.

"They only do that in movies," she hissed and made a grab for him.

She was too late. He sprinted off in the direction of the shooter and stood behind a telephone pole. Another building was beside the import-export loading dock, and that one also had a large parking area with pillars and ramps. Richie headed for it.

With a curse, she followed. Spotting a smashed beer can, she grabbed and tossed the can far as she could toward her right, hoping the sound as it landed would draw fire and she'd be able to spot the gunman.

It didn't.

She scrambled after Richie. She had no idea where he'd disappeared to, only that he needed some protection ... and she needed to catch a killer.

She heard a "thump" then an "Oomph!" followed by another "whack, thump, blam." Quickly, she followed the sounds. Two men held Richie while Punk Leo pummeled him ... again.

She stretched out her arms, a two-handed grip on her gun. "Stop right now, Leo!" she shouted loud to make herself heard over the swearing, punching, and Richie's grunts of pain. "I don't miss when I shoot!"

Leo's arm was high when he looked over and saw the barrel of a powerful Glock facing him. It wasn't some wimpy twenty-two. It was big. A cop's gun.

The two guys with him decided to show respect for a serious firearm. They let go of Richie and ran. She let them go. It was Leo she was after.

"So, your girlfriend's a cop," he said, his voice sneering as he faced Richie who was sitting on the ground rubbing his ribs and stomach. "What were you thinking bringing a cop to my house? Here, to my business? I told you to keep away from me, but you wouldn't listen! This isn't over, Richie."

"Yes, it is," Rebecca said, showing her badge. "I'm bringing you in for questioning about the death of"—she hesitated, but it was the only name she knew—"Cockeyed Lanigan. You're not under arrest yet, but you come quietly or you'll be charged with assault and battery."

"I didn't hurt Lanigan! I was trying to stop him from ..." Suddenly, he shut his mouth. "I know nothing. I want to talk to my lawyer. I won't answer any more questions."

She knew enough about the law and lawyers to know there was no way she was going to be allowed to interrogate Leo on Christmas Eve after he'd asked for a lawyer. Probably not Christmas Day, either. She didn't have enough probable cause to go after an arrest warrant. Not yet, anyway. "You'll have plenty of chance for that," she said. Let him stew awhile, she thought, as she turned her attention on Richie. "Are you all right? Do you want to go to a hospital?"

"I don't need a hospital." He got up and walked to her side as he felt the damage done to his bleeding lip. "I just need my handkerchief back. And I want Leo to tell me where the old Santas are." He faced Leo. "I know you know about them."

"Sure," Leo said eying the two. "I just got a couple of kid's bikes and I need to make a delivery for them. That's why I'm out here and saw you two sneaking around my warehouse. Why?" Slowly the light seemed to dawn. "Is that what this is about? You're trying to find them? You're the transport, right? And you lost them." He chuckled. "I was wondering about that. Well, I'll be damned!"

"Where are they?" Richie demanded again.

Leo folded his arms. "No way, Richie. You ruin my Christmas, I'll ruin yours."

"Damn you!" Richie moved forward.

Rebecca put an arm out, stopping him.

"Eat me," Leo said with a nasty smirk.

"Cool it, you two." Rebecca put her gun in the handbag and handed Richie the handkerchief, then faced Leo. "Why did you shoot at us? And why beat up Richie?"

He looked disgusted. "The first was to scare you away. How was I supposed to know who it was around my warehouse? The second was to show what happens to somebody too stupid to run after being shot at. Officially, however, I thought he was a burglar."

Rebecca had to admit to a certain logic to that. "I'll let you go tonight, but stay close to home and to your phone. We can talk tomorrow—"

"But it's Christmas!"

"At eleven in the morning. Have your attorney call me. And don't forget. I don't like it when people forget to do what I tell them."

Even in the dark, she could see Leo turn pale. She knew his attorney would call and say he and Leo couldn't be there until December 26th at earliest, but it was okay. Leo wasn't going anywhere, and her gut feeling told her he wasn't a murderer.

Crooked, yes. Murderer, no.

She did suspect, however, that he knew a lot more about the dead Santa than he was willing to say without some major threats. Too much "coincidence" was going on here. Once she got Punk Leo and his attorney into the intimidating location otherwise known as Homicide's interrogation room, she felt pretty certain he would open up. "What is it they call you?" she asked, directing her question at her so-so suspect. "Punk Leo? Very appropriate, if you ask me. Get out of here now."

He ran to his car, casting aspersions on Richie's manhood the entire way.

7

ANGIE AMALFI LOOKED AT the clock when she heard the knock on her apartment door. It was early for Paavo and besides, the knock was too quiet for him. He had a cop's "open up or else" knock, even when coming to see her. They were going to go to dinner and then to her parents' house for Christmas Eve.

Angie was a petite woman with wavy brown hair streaked with light auburn highlights. She'd been looking forward to this Christmas Eve for some time—the first one for her and Paavo as an engaged couple.

She opened the door, then her mouth dropped and she stared. Was this a joke? Her mother, Serefina Amalfi, stood in front of her dressed up like a vision of a very w-i-i-d-e sugar plum fairy wearing a Christmasy red dress decorated with large white polka dots, her black coat haphazardly tossed over one arm. Springs of mistletoe formed a corsage. Serefina's cheeks were fiery red. She'd obviously been testing the eggnog.

That wasn't the whole story, though. Behind her were more little old Santa Clauses than Angie had ever seen. "What's going on, Mamma?" she asked, wide-eyed. "Did you raid the North Pole?"

"These are my good friends," Serefina's words slurred as she linked arms with two of them. Her coat fell and Angie picked it up. "We've been celebrating, talking about the good old days. And we have a favor to ask of you."

"Where's Papà?" she asked, sticking her head out the door to better see through the blaze of red.

Just then, her neighbor Stan Bonnette, probably because of all the commotion, opened his apartment door, gazed into the hall at the plethora of Christmas spirit, gawked, and then quickly shut the door again. His dead bolt clicked into place.

"Your papà is home," Serefina answered. "He's waiting for us, the old fart. He doesn't like to go out, as you know." She lowered her voice to a stage whisper. "And he doesn't approve of all my friends." She put a finger in front of her mouth and said, "Shush."

"Mamma, I think you need some coffee," Angie said, pulling her inside.

"Your father is such an old man!" Serefina wailed. "Not like *miei amici!*" To Angie, her mother's friends looked eighty at youngest. "So, are you going to make them stand in the hallway, or are you going to help us?"

Angie instinctively put her arms up to block the door. It was Christmas Eve and Paavo was coming over soon for their private celebration. This couldn't be happening. With brows creased, she asked suspiciously, "Help you with what, Mamma?"

After Richie's lip stopped bleeding, he looked at his watch. It was after eight. "Damn! I've got to get going."

"Drop me off at Homicide?" she asked.

"Sure."

They rode in silence except for the time he asked her what she was looking for in her purse. She told him it was her key card to get into Homicide after hours. Actually, it was one half of a homing device that she planned to stick under the Porsche's passenger seat. The other half remained in her purse. She wasn't about to let him ride off, possibly to meet with the killer she was looking for, without doing anything about it. She could tell from the way he drove, constantly checking side and rearview mirrors, that he was far too paranoid about being followed for her to tail him the normal way.

The magnet on the homer make a little "dink" as it met the metal bars under the seat and she coughed, trying to cover the sound. He glanced her way. She patted her chest. "Sorry."

"Look, Inspector," he said, "I'm sorry about this, too. The day didn't go quite the way I'd planned. I didn't mean to put you in danger. Or myself, for that matter."

"I know. For me, it goes with the territory."

He stopped just outside the Hall of Justice parking lot. Her seven year old Ford Explorer with four-wheel drive, a V8 engine, and a CD player, perfect for when she went up to the mountains or to some remote beach for vacation, was the only auto remaining in the center of the lot. A couple of security guard cars were right next to the building.

"Looks like just about everyone's gone home for Christmas Eve," she said.

"Yeah. Guess so," he murmured, facing her. "Rebecca—"

She immediately opened the car door and practically jumped out of the Porsche. "See you around, Richie Amalfi."

His dark eyes perused hers and held a moment, but then he simply nodded. "Okay. Be careful out there, Inspector."

"Will do." With that, she shut the door, and he drove off.

Hurrying to her car, she set up her half of the homing device on the dashboard. It whirred for a moment, not doing a thing, then began a steady, pulsating beep. Success!

She started out, heading left as she'd seen him go. She'd ridden with others as they'd used one of these devices to follow a suspect, but she'd never done it on her own and it was trickier than she'd imagined. Richie would turn a corner, and she'd go straight, only to realize her mistake when the beeps grew weak and slow. It'd be a matter of U-turning when possible, if not racing madly around a block to pick up the strong steady pulse once again.

To her surprise, he drove to the hilly high-rent area in the center of the city known as Twin Peaks. They zigged and zagged their way up its curvy streets and were nearing the top when the beeps stopped completely.

How could she have lost him here? Rebecca wondered. She slowed to a crawl and continued to drive along the winding roads with its many smaller side streets and dead ends.

Soon, she reached the very top of the hill. If he came up here, he must have had a destination in mind. But what? Who?

She slowly traveled along the streets, driving around and around, in and out of side streets and cul-de-sacs, listening for a ping, and looking for his car. Maybe he lived here and had pulled into his garage. But the homing device would still beep.

What if he realized what she had done? And then led her here to a wild goose chase? He might have disabled the device, knowing she would waste her time driving in circles, just as she had done, and...

Was that a ping?

She froze, listening. Then she heard another ... and another. They seemed to be coming a bit faster, a bit louder, which meant he was approaching. She shut off the car's lights then backed off the street she was on into a small side street and waited.

The homing device grew louder and less than twenty

seconds later, Richie's black Porsche flew down the street, leaving Twin Peaks behind.

As best she could, she followed.

Presidio Heights was an area filled with mansions of the rich and famous, including politicians and some of the top medical specialists and lawyers in the country. She expected Richie to drive straight through it and keep going, when the beeps began to grow faster and faster.

He must have stopped, she thought. But why here?

She pulled over. This was one of the few parts of the city with street parking readily available. It was because there were few apartment dwellers vying for space, and many of the mansions had added underground parking to keep the owners' expensive cars safe from the elements and thieves. For a moment, she could scarcely believe she was still in San Francisco.

She got out of the Explorer and hurried to the street corner to look for Richie's car.

To the right, in the center of the block was a brightly lit mansion with many cars parked nearby, the Porsche among them.

She phoned dispatch to find out who lived in the house. To her surprise, the answer wasn't readily available. A search had to be performed before she got a name: Giorgio Boiardi.

"My God," she muttered. The name was familiar. She took Richie's iPad mini out of her purse and prayed its wireless Internet would work in this area.

It connected. Within seconds, Google verified her memory and added to it. Giorgio Boiardi, mobster, headed West Coast operation 1959-1988, in prison 1989-2005 when released due to old age and infirmity.

Curious, she searched for his birth date, and when she found it, looked again to make sure she was reading it right. He was born exactly ninety years ago. It was his birthday!

This must be a birthday party. And all the old men ... could they all have been ...?

She had to swallow hard. Had she stumbled upon a group of old criminals gathering in one place to celebrate the birthday of the *capo di tutti capi*? The Don? Is that what was happening?

No wonder Richie wouldn't tell her what was going on. How many of the guys he was looking for had outstanding warrants? How many could she pull in to finally serve time for the crimes they'd committed? That was the reason for the Santa suits. Not that they were a bunch of do-gooders, but because they were wanted men! They needed to hide their faces. What better way than as Santa Claus the day before Christmas?

And Richie Amalfi was in the middle of it all. The big softie was trying to help old men—old *crooked* men—to have one more birthday and Christmas celebration together. She shook her head at the thought.

Now what? One person who was a cop and yet understood the Amalfis came to mind—Paavo Smith. They needed to talk. She tried his cell phone, but it went straight to messaging.

Intuition sparked and she flipped through the stored addresses on her cell phone.

A cheerful, feminine voice answered the call. A few minutes of conversation yielded more information—and surprises— than she ever imagined.

She sped across the city. The city was tiny, but between traffic jams and traffic lights, it could easily take a half hour to go a few miles. Fortunately, on Christmas Eve, even in San Francisco, the streets were fairly empty.

Most people were home or visiting friends and families, not racing around hoping to make a career-establishing, big time arrest.

When she reached her destination, she saw the white Econoline parked across the street. She all but rubbed her hands in glee. She was on the right track after all.

Impatiently, she waited for the elevator to bring her up to the top floor of the apartment building. She had never been there before, but she heard about it often enough to know not only how to find the building, but exactly what it would look like inside.

The door opened. Angelina Amalfi looked prettier than ever in a red silk dress with matching shoes and gold and pearl jewelry. Rebecca had never even owned dyed-to-match shoes. She felt frumpy as she realized what her once white blouse and crisp black slacks must look like after the day's exertions. And she'd never even put the barrette back in her hair. She buttoned her jacket, hoping that might help.

"Come in," Angie said. "We've got eggnog and lots of cookies. The last batch of biscotti is still baking—and Paavo's back from the grocery now, too. We used a lot of sugar tonight."

Rebecca's gaze swept over the apartment taking in everything at once, and all but gasping by what she saw. The living room was much more attractive than she expected it would be. The furniture was a mixture of antique and modern. She had imagined it would be gaudy with dark wood and Victorian curlicues as far as the eye could see. Instead, it was light and peaceful, much simpler and more tasteful than she had thought ... or, than she had hoped.

Santas sat around the dining room table, on the petit-point sofa, antique Hepplewhite chair, and across the room on a pair of wingbacks. A couple of them stood in the kitchen. They still wore their suits, but their hats and beards were off. Even sitting, she could tell that most of them were stooped and frail. Perhaps once large and forceful, they were now quite elderly.

Finally, her gaze settled on that of her fellow inspector. Paavo was standing in the dining area talking to a heavy-set older woman. He excused himself and approached, a drink in one hand, the sleeves on his white shirt rolled back, his tie slightly loosened, and with a smidgeon of flour on his brown slacks. He looked relaxed and ... happy. Not the stern, serious man he always was at work. Her heart contracted.

"What's the problem, Rebecca?" he asked, knowing she wasn't there on a social call. "I heard you were looking for me."

Earlier, when she called simply to ask for Paavo to talk over with him all she had learned, she could hardly believe what Angie told her—fortunately, Angie was a bit of a chatterbox. That was what brought her to Angie's apartment.

She came rushing over here because she had a duty to perform, but now, she wondered about the wisdom of doing it.

"I ... um ..." She looked from one Santa to the other. Canes were everywhere. At least no one used a walker. Hauling them all into jail was going to be a bit more awkward than she'd imagined. She lowered her voice. "I've got to question the old Santas about a strange death I'm investigating—a death of another old Santa!"

"I see," Paavo said with a grimace. He understood her problem. "Do you think they're involved?"

"Not really, but they very probably have information I could use."

"They were planning to go somewhere for a Christmas Eve party, although I get the feeling none of them know how to get there."

"Really? I believe I know exactly where the party is," she said.

"Sounds like you've got a bargaining chip," Paavo told her with a nod.

Rebecca faced the group and asked for their attention. She began by introducing herself, then said, "I'm sorry to inform you that Cockeyed Lanigan was killed this morning. I'm here to ask if any of you can help in my investigation of his death."

Joe the Pistol turned to Serefina with a scowl. "If I'da known you was so chummy with all these cops, I never woulda called you!"

The others told him to shush.

Rebecca knew what was going on: they'd spent a lifetime learning not to talk to or trust a cop. "Listen, I know where you're supposed to be tonight," she said. "And I can take you there, but not until I learn something about Cockeyed Lanigan. Now, who wants to start?"

As one, they all turned their backs on her as they began to put on their beards and hats.

"I don't know why I'm bothering with this get-up," Lorenzo the Slug muttered to Guido Cucumber. "We're already at a goddamned cop convention."

"Damn right," the Cucumber said with a sneer. "We gotta get the hell outta here!"

"Hold it, everyone," Paavo said. "Rebecca's okay. She just needs answers to a few questions."

"Easy for you to say," Joey Zoom grumped.

"Wait! He's my son-in-law to be," Serefina protested. "You trust me, you trust Paavo."

"We trust Paavo. Just not *her*." Joey Zoom waved his thumb at Rebecca. "She comes here threatening. The hell with that!"

Rebecca realized the folly of her completely wrong approach with these men. "Look, I've just got a couple of questions."

"Tell the girl," Serefina urged. "Nobody liked Cockeyed anyway, so why not tell her about him?"

The Santas eyed each other.

Finally, Joey the Pistol spoke. "Okay, if you really want to know. Cockeyed was bad. Word was he hated a Big Somebody. Real big. Maybe he wanted to ice that Somebody. Thought he could follow us around, find out where the party was, and then sneak in wearing a Santa suit. Now, I ain't saying that's what was going to happen, but it might be what he planned."

The others nodded.

Rebecca didn't buy it. "So Cockeyed was going to somehow use you guys to get to this Big Somebody, but then he just happened to get himself killed?"

The Santas all shifted nervously. "Look, we saw Cockeyed following us when we was out at the airport," Lorenzo the Slug said. "Joey Zoom took care of the van so we'd get rid of Richie. But then, when Joey Zoom pulled off the freeway, Cockeyed tried to follow. But it seems he made a little mistake and drove off the overpass instead."

"He did what?"

At Rebecca's startled expression, Joey the Pistol explained, "Cockeyed didn't get his nickname for nothing! Nobody wanted to ride with him driving, not ever. We figured he musta got rattled, and did a swan dive."

The others agreed, some loudly.

Rebecca and Paavo traded glances. "Wait a minute!" she said. "If Cockeyed's death was an accident that happened right near the airport, how did he end up miles away in the middle of the Stonestown Mall?"

The Santas all turned expectedly to Joey Zoom. "As I see it" he said, "Punk Leo spilled the beans to Cockeyed about Big Somebody's birthday party and about us with our Santa suits so nobody would recognize us. But then Punk Leo must have got wind of Cockeyed's plans to get even with Big Somebody. He realized if Cockeyed hurt the big man, then Leo would be toast. So, Leo followed Cockeyed to try to stop him. He musta seen when poor Cockeyed was called by His Maker. Maybe it scared him, who knows, and he didn't want to leave the body where there might be questions about Cockeyed wearing a Santa suit. Word could get out, you know, and Big Somebody—well, let's just say he's good at puttin' two and two together."

Rebecca was having some difficulty with all the ins, outs, and innuendos, but she followed the gist of what Joey was telling her. She nodded.

Joey Zoom continued. "Punk Leo probably figured out a way to get ridda the body. But with all the security guards at the mall, he got cold feet and stuffed the body someplace hoping to get it later. But he didn't hide it so good, and it got found."

"Or," Guido said, "since a lotta things Punk Leo handles, he gets 'cause they fall outta a truck, maybe Cockeyed *really* fell outta a truck, and that's how he ended up where he did."

The old Santa all chuckled at that observation.

"Isn't that sweet?" Serefina said, clasping her hands to her ample breasts. "Punk Leo saved *il cap—*, I mean, Big Somebody from Cockeyed and only disturbed the accident scene because he wanted to help. *Madonna mia*, what a dear boy!"

Rebecca gawked at her.

Twelve Santa heads bobbed up and down in agreement.

Paavo looked at Rebecca and shrugged as if to say, "Could be."

Rebecca took a deep breath. Punk Leo did a lot he shouldn't have ... moving the body from the scene of an accident to start with, and then having that body tumble off his transportation to land in the middle of a parking lot. But if Cockeyed was actually killed in an automobile accident, murder wasn't one of Punk Leo's multitude of sins.

And that meant, it wasn't a homicide, and therefore not Rebecca's problem. Whatever Leo was charged with, if anything, would be up to D.A. and Leo's lawyers to sort out.

As for the old Santas, she probably could haul all of them

down to City Jail on some pretext—reckless driving, if nothing else—and see if any outstanding warrants turned up.

Her eyes strayed to the beautiful Christmas tree in one corner of the living room as her mind replayed the scene of Richie and her in Union Square earlier that day, watching the shoppers and tourists, listening to Christmas carols ...

And something loosened in her heart. She looked at Paavo who was regarding her steadily, trusting her judgment, and then at Serefina's anxious face.

"One more question," she said to the group. "One thing I don't understand. Since Richie Amalfi was your driver, why did you run off and leave him?"

"Why not?" Lorenzo the Slug wrinkled his mouth in disgust. "He was a pain in the ass, thinking he had to baby us, watch out for us, tell us to do this, do that. We've taken care of ourselves for eighty years and don't need some young punk doing it now! Besides, we wanted to get a present for a dear friend who's celebrating his birthday today. Something that money can't buy, and I think we've got it."

Angie took that opportunity to carry from the kitchen a big Italian hand-painted pasta bowl filled with just-from-the-oven biscotti, amaretti and honey-dipped cookies. The whole thing was wrapped in green cellophane, gathered at the top to form a flowery design and tied with an enormous green ribbon. "Here it is!" she cried.

The old men who were still awake cheered. The others woke from the noise and cheered as well, eventually.

Rebecca knew what she had to do.

8

REBECCA WAITED FOR what seemed like a century on the doorstep after speaking with an immaculate butler.

The door reopened and Richie appeared, his gaze questioning. She noticed that he now wore a tuxedo with a black bowtie instead of the probably ruined suit he had been wearing earlier. That must have been the reason for his quick trip up Twin Peaks.

"I have a Christmas present for you," she said with a smile, and then stepped aside.

His expression was indescribable as his gaze traveled from the twelve Santas, to the cookies, and then to Rebecca. His face spread into a wide smile. "Come on in, guys. Everybody's waiting for you." He stood back, and the Santas entered, single-file, to loud greetings and cheers.

He and Rebecca remained alone in the doorway. The smile he wore was now for her alone, and she couldn't help but notice that he had a very nice smile, one that reached his eyes. "Where'd you find them?"

She grinned. "They were baking cookies."

Dark eyes met hers. "You've saved my life! Do you realize what the reaction would have been if I told the birthday boy I'd lost his twelve best friends?" He shuddered. "I kept saying they were on their way ... and then said three Hail Mary's for it to come true. This is, like, a miracle."

She took a little bow. "Glad to be of service."

Laughter from the party erupted, and the two of them laughed as well. In the background, Sinatra sang *"Winter Wonderland."*

"Rebecca," Richie said, pointedly not using Inspector Mayfield, "come on inside with me. It's Christmas Eve. Join the party."

The air was cool and crisp, the night a velvet canvas filled with stars. Inside were warm lights and happy sounds of the party. It was tempting, she had to admit. Looking at him there dressed so nicely, he looked handsome and a bit too tempting as well. She found an excuse to say no. "I'm on call tonight."

"There are plenty of non-alcoholic drinks. And you might not get any call."

"I'm not exactly dressed for a party," she said, looking at her wrinkled and dirty outfit.

"It doesn't matter at all."

She met his eyes. "I'd rather not, for a number of reasons," she said. "You, on the other hand, look very nice." She reached out and straightened his bowtie. "Enjoy the party."

He took hold of her hand. "How can I convince you to stay?"

His hand was warm, hard and masculine. Thoughts of their crazy adventure filled her, running up and down the streets of Chinatown, him sitting on a curb as she ranted at him, him fighting with Punk Leo in the kitchen.

She pulled away her hand. "You can't." She turned and walked down the steps to the sidewalk.

"It's Christmas Eve," he said, hurrying down to her side. "It's not a time to be alone."

"You've got a party to go to."

"To watch a bunch of people who have spent years together share their memories?" he said wryly. He took her arm, stopping her. "Maybe I'd rather create some memories of my own, if you don't mind my company as you wait to see if any police dispatcher's call comes in tonight."

She looked at the long, dark sidewalk that led to her SUV. She could walk it alone, and then sit in an empty office, or go home alone to her apartment. He wasn't anyone she should ever get involved with. They were from two different worlds. Actually, more like two different universes. Still, a surprising stab of regret hit her as she shook her head and whispered, "Merry Christmas, Richie."

"You've got to admit," he said as he slid his hands in his pockets and continued to walk with her. "This day was pretty crazy."

"Yes, it was," she agreed.

"Poor Cockeyed Lanigan," he murmured. "And my old Santas getting lost."

"Lost?" She glanced at him. "They were never lost. They ditched you!"

His face fell. "They did what?"

"You heard me. They said you mother-henned them too much. They couldn't take it." She laughed.

He looked so stricken. "You think that's funny? All they put me through!"

She laughed harder.

"I'll tell them a thing or two!" He turned towards the house.

"No, no!" She grabbed his arm. "I shouldn't have told you."

He faced her, her hand still holding onto him, and as their

eyes met, his anger and her laugher died. "Maybe I did kind of overdo watching them," he said with a shrug.

"Maybe, a little." She dropped her hand, but this time didn't turn away.

He watched her a moment, then said, "I was just thinking, Punk Leo interrupted the only food we had all day, and I'm starving. I have friends who own a restaurant in Chinatown that stays open all night. I think they're Buddhists, so they stay open on Christmas Eve. What do you say? Even on-call, you've got to eat."

She knew that tomorrow she would decide this was a big mistake, and would most likely never see him again, but for tonight ... just tonight ... he was right. She didn't want to be alone, and clearly, even though he had a party to go to, neither did he.

"Come to think of it," she said. "I am hungry."

"Great! And if no calls came in for you, I know a movie house that's playing old Christmas movies all night long."

"Really? I love old movies," she said.

"Me, too." Both looked surprised that they finally found something to agree on.

"*It's a Wonderful Life* is one of my favorites this time of year," she added.

His mouth wrinkled. "God, no! It's so syrupy! *Santa Clause Conquers the Martians*—now *that's* a fun movie to watch!"

"You've *got* to be joking," she said.

"Dead serious."

"You'll be dead, all right, if you expect me to spend Christmas Eve watching that dreck."

"Or," he said, "maybe we'll find something more interesting to do."

As her eyebrows rose, he tucked her hand in the crook of his arm and walked her to his Porsche, and soon they drove off to what would surely be a most unforgettable Christmas.

#

*I hope you enjoyed THE THIRTEENTH SANTA. The adventures of Rebecca and Richie continue in **ONE O'CLOCK HUSTLE**, their first full-length mystery. Once you begin the Rebecca Mayfield mysteries, the hours just seem to fly by.*

One O'Clock Hustle

AT 1:05 A.M. ON Sunday morning, after working twenty-four hours straight on the capture of an armed suspect in the murder of a liquor store clerk, Inspector Rebecca Mayfield sat alone at her desk in Homicide.

She was exhausted. But just as she finished writing up her notes on the tension-filled arrest, ready to head home for some much-needed sleep, the police dispatcher called: a shooting, one fatality, reported at Big Caesar's Nightclub.

Rebecca had heard of the club, located in San Francisco's touristy North Beach area. She was the first investigator to arrive at the scene and flashed her badge at the uniformed police officer at the door. "Mayfield. Homicide."

"Good news," Officer Danzig said, all but beaming. "We're holding the killer. The bouncers caught him. He clammed up right away, but you'll find him in the manager's office."

Rebecca's eyebrows rose. She had never had witnesses capture the suspect before. "Interesting. And good; very good." Maybe she would get some sleep tonight after all.

"His name is ..." the officer pulled out his notepad and read from it, "Richard Amalfi."

Rebecca was suddenly jolted wide awake. "What did you say?"

"Richard Amalfi. He's well known at the club, apparently comes here frequently. Everyone calls him Richie."

It can't be. Her mouth went dry. "I see." There are a lot of Amalfis in this city, she told herself. "Did you see him?"

"I did. Not quite six feet, medium build, black hair, late thirties or early forties."

Damn. That sounded like the Richie Amalfi she knew. He was quite a character to be sure, but a murderer? The thought jarred her. She shook her head, needing to focus on the crime, on doing her job. "What do we know about the victim?"

"No name yet. Female, in her thirties, I'd say. We only know she was a customer. Apparently she came in with the man who killed her."

"Allegedly killed her," Rebecca automatically added.

"Allegedly," Danzig repeated. "Although they said he was caught in the act. The body's in the bookkeeper's office."

Caught in the act ... The words reverberated round and round in her head as she tried to listen to a run-down of the club's layout—the ballroom straight ahead, the coat closet and restrooms to the left, and beyond them, cordoned off with yellow tape, the corridor with the manager's office where Richie was being held, and the bookkeeper's office where the murder took place.

"Was the victim connected to the bookkeeper in some way?" she asked.

"No one has said. The bookkeeper isn't here this time of night."

Rebecca would have been shocked if he was. Nine-to-fivers liked their beauty sleep.

Danzig went on to assure her that he and his partner had immediately shut down the club and no one had been allowed to enter or leave.

She thanked the officer and stepped away from him, drawing a deep breath as she thought of all that was to come.

If Homicide were a family, Richie Amalfi would be a close relative. Rebecca's favorite co-worker, Inspector Paavo Smith, was engaged to Richie's cousin, Angelina Amalfi.

From Paavo, she knew Richie could come up with just about anything that anyone might want. Need something big, small, expensive, cheap, common, or rare? It didn't matter. Cousin Richie could provide. Many people seemed to "know a guy who knows a guy." Well, Richie was that guy—the one people went to when they needed something. She didn't want to get into what that "something" might be, or the legality of how he got it. But that didn't make him a killer ... she hoped.

She entered the elegant ballroom with white cloth-covered tables forming a semi-circle around an empty dance floor. She had never been there before—beer and pizza were her speed; jeans, turtleneck sweaters, black leather jackets, and boots her style.

The popular nightspot had been designed to look like a glamorous nightclub from the forties, the sort of place where Sinatra, Tony Bennett or Dean Martin might have sung, where women dressed in glittery gowns, men wore black or white jackets with bow ties, and "dancing cheek-to-cheek" referred to the couple's faces, not other parts of the anatomy. No hip-hop, rap or, God-forbid, country-western would ever be performed at Big Caesar's.

She could absolutely see Richie in a place like this—as absolutely as she couldn't see him killing anyone. Yet he was "caught in the act," the police officer had said.

As much as she didn't want to believe it, she needed to put aside her personal feelings. She had no more reason to believe he was innocent than she did anyone else accused of a crime. And yet ...

And yet, she couldn't help but remember the day, last Christmas Eve, when she worked alone in Homicide and he came in looking for Paavo for help with a problem. Paavo was off duty, so she ended up helping, and had spent the day and well into the night with him, finally heading home in the early hours of Christmas morning. Their time together hadn't been long, but it had been intense, including chases and shootouts, and the kind of life and death struggles—crazy though they were—that left emotions raw and defenses down. To her amazement, she had enjoyed being with him.

She then used the next several days wondering if she'd been stupid to have spent so much time with him.

Not that anything had "happened" between them. Heaven forbid! After all, from the moment she first met him, she knew he wasn't her type, and he clearly realized the same about her. Still, from time to time, she couldn't help but wonder ...

In any case, he never contacted her again—which told her that the only thing stupid was to have wasted any time whatsoever thinking about him. Of course, if he had called and asked her out, she would have refused to go. She wondered if he hadn't realized that. He was, she had discovered, curiously perceptive.

The band now jauntily played *The Best is Yet to Come,* but a sullen, wary mood blanketed the room.

When she left the ballroom, she found that her partner, Bill Sutter, had arrived. He was taking statements from the bouncers. Rebecca walked around to get a quick feel for the nightclub's layout and exits, both doors and windows.

Despite wanting to see and question Richie, she would save him for last.

From her several years of experience in Homicide, she knew

that the more she learned about a situation the better her first questions would be, and the better she could judge the veracity of a suspect's answers. Since she knew the alleged "perp," she was going to have to be even more by-the-book in this case than she normally was.

She ducked under the yellow crime scene tape. A cop stood at the door of one of the offices.

"Homicide," Rebecca said as she put on latex gloves and entered the office. The victim lay face up in the center of the room.

She appeared to be in her early thirties and to Rebecca's eye the sort of blonde—beautiful, slim, and expensively dressed—that fit easily in a classy place like Big Caesar's; the sort of woman she could imagine Richie going out with.

A gunshot had struck her heart. Death was most likely instantaneous or close to it. Blood soaked the carpet beneath her.

Rebecca surveyed the rest of the room. The window was open wide, bringing in blustery, cold air. Piles of papers lay in a wind-tossed jumble across the desk where a brass nameplate read "Daniel Pasternak." Behind it hung a sappy Thomas Kincaid painting of little sparkling pastel-colored cottages ready-made for Disney's seven dwarfs. On the floor near the body lay a small satin handbag.

Rebecca picked it up and opened it. The bag was empty except for two twenties and a lipstick. No cell phone; no credit cards. That was surprising, and odd.

Just then, the medical examiner, Evelyn Ramirez, arrived. She wore a red sequined blouse, black silk slacks, and diamonds. Her black hair was pulled back tight and pinned up in a sleek chignon. She had obviously been called away from some big shindig and intended to return to it soon.

The ME quickly took in the body and its surroundings. "Well, this'll be fast."

Rebecca watched Ramirez do the preliminary examination to make sure no big surprises turned up—such as the corpse had actually been dead for twelve hours before someone found her, not twenty seconds like everyone said. The entry wound indicated the shot had been fired at close range, a few feet away, which was consistent with the killer and victim being together in the room.

With the exam concluded, the time had come for Rebecca to face Richie.

She took a deep breath and opened the door to the office of the nightclub manager.

Richie stood at the window, his back to her, looking into the night. His wrists were handcuffed behind him.

Two cops sat near the desk—a desk overflowing with paper-work. When Rebecca entered, they walked over to the door and stood beside it.

Richie slowly turned and faced her. Even in handcuffs he seemed calm, cool, and suave in a black jacket, white shirt, and black bow tie, almost like something out of a James Bond movie. Or, more in keeping with him and his friends, *The Godfather*.

"Richie Amalfi," she whispered.

He took a step towards her, then stopped, his deep-set, heavy-lidded brown eyes troubled and questioning. As he gazed at her, she saw something else in them, but she wasn't sure what.

She steeled herself and raised her head high, giving him a cold, icy stare.

His shoulders seemed to sag at that. "Rebecca Rulebook," he murmured, then pushed a noisy breath past his lips, and wryly shook his head. "Guess I should kiss my ass goodbye."

His saying that, his thinking that way about her, momen-tarily stung, but she pushed the feelings aside and concentrated on the job before her. She pulled out a chair for Richie, and then another for herself facing it. Truth be told, she moved the furniture around to give herself time to think, and to give her breathing a chance to return to normal.

"Have a seat, Richie." She prided herself on being a cop. Raised in Idaho, she had always followed the straight and narrow, and believed that all God's children were created equally. But if one of them got out of line, the full power of the law should stomp down until they saw the light. And Richie Amalfi was no exception.

Continue with ONE O'CLOCK HUSTLE ...

ABOUT THE AUTHOR

Joanne Pence was born and raised in northern California. She is an award-winning, *USA Today* best-selling author of mysteries, and has written historical fiction, contemporary romance, romantic suspense, and ghostly romances. She also holds a master's degree in journalism from U.C. Berkeley.

Joanne's stories travel across times and places, blending suspense, emotion, and the occasional touch of humor—perfect for readers who love being surprised by where a story can take them. All of her books are available in ebook and print, with many also offered in large print and audiobook editions. Visit her at **Joannepence [dot] com** and sign up for her mailing list to be the first to hear about new releases and behind-the-scenes news.

Contemporary, Historical and Fantasy Novels

Seems Like Old Times
When Lee Reynolds, nationally known television news anchor, returns to the small town where she was born to sell her now-vacant childhood home, little does she expect to find that her first love has moved back to town. Nor does she expect that her feelings for him are still so strong.

Tony Santos had been a major league baseball player, but now finds his days of glory gone. He's gone back home to raise his young son as a single dad.

Both Tony and Lee have changed a lot. Yet, being with him, she finds that in her heart, it seems like old times…

Dangerous Journey

Set in 1978, when Hong Kong was still a British Crown Colony, C.J. Perkins arrives in the maze of the city searching for her brother, who vanished during a Peace Corps assignment. She's chasing the only lead she has—a whisper about something called the White Dragon. The authorities dismiss her questions, the Peace Corps offers regrets instead of answers, and every door she knocks on seems to close in her face.

Her only real option is Darius Kane: adventurer, bounty hunter, and the kind of man who knows how to survive in the shadows between law and crime. C.J. practically shanghais him into the search, forcing an uneasy partnership neither of them wants—but both of them need.

C.J. and Darius follow a trail that takes them through the narrow streets of Hong Kong, the backrooms of San Francisco's Chinatown, and the wild jungles of Borneo as they pursue both her brother and the White Dragon. The closer C.J. gets to them, the more danger she finds herself in—and it's not just danger of losing her life, but also of losing her heart.

Dance with a Gunfighter

Willa Cather Literary Award finalist for Best Historical Novel

Set in the lawless Arizona Territory of the 1870s, Gabriella Devere sets out to avenge her family's murder after a gang of outlaws leaves her with nothing but grief. With no help from the authorities, she rides into outlaw country alone, determined to make the men who destroyed her life answer for their sins.

Jess McLowry left his war-torn Southern home to head West, where he hired out his gun. When he learns what happened to Gabriella's family, and what she plans, he knows a young woman like her will have no chance against the outlaws, and vows to save her the way he couldn't save his own family.

But the price of vengeance is high and Gabriella's willingness to sacrifice everything ultimately leads to the book's deadly and startling conclusion.

The Ghost of Squire House

For decades, the home built by reclusive artist, Paul Squire, has stood empty on a windswept cliff overlooking the ocean. Those who attempted to live in the home soon fled in terror. Jennifer Barrett knows nothing of the history of the house she inherited. All she knows is she's glad for the chance to make a new life for herself.

A compelling, prickly ghost with a tortured, guilt-ridden past, and a lonely heroine determined to start fresh, find themselves in a battle of wills and emotion in this ghostly fantasy of love, time, and chance.

The Dragon's Lady

Turn-of-the-century San Francisco comes to life in this romance of star-crossed lovers whose love is forbidden by both society and the laws of the time.

Ruth Greer, wealthy daughter of a shipping magnate, finds a young boy who has run away from his home in Chinatown—an area of gambling parlors, opium dens, and sing-song girls, as well as families trying to eke out a living. It is also home to the infamous and deadly "hatchet men" of Chinese lore.

There, Ruth meets Li Han-lin, a handsome, enigmatic leader of one such tong. The two are from completely different worlds, and when both worlds are shattered by the Great Earthquake and Fire of 1906 that destroyed most of San Francisco, they face their ultimate test.

The Donnelly Cabin Inn Series

Three half-sisters inherit a remote cabin, but there's just one problem with it. It's haunted.

IF I LOVED YOU

THIS CAN'T BE LOVE

SENTIMENTAL JOURNEY

A CERTAIN SMILE

TIME AFTER TIME

The Rebecca Mayfield Mysteries

Rebecca is a by-the-book detective, who walks the straight and narrow in her work, and in her life. Richie, on the other hand, is not at all by-the-book. But opposites can and do attract, and there are few mystery two-somes quite as opposite as Rebecca and Richie.

ONE O'CLOCK HUSTLE – North American Book Award winner in Mystery

TWO O'CLOCK HEIST

THREE O'CLOCK SÉANCE

FOUR O'CLOCK SIZZLE

FIVE O'CLOCK TWIST

SIX O'CLOCK SILENCE

SEVEN O'CLOCK TARGET

EIGHT O'CLOCK SPLIT

NINE O'CLOCK RETREAT

Plus a Christmas Novella: The Thirteenth Santa

The Cook and Inspector Mysteries

Gourmet cook Angie Amalfi and San Francisco Homicide Inspector Paavo Smith face crime and calories in this now complete mystery series:

DEATH ON A SILVER PLATTER

A QUICHE BEFORE DYING

THE MARINARA MURDERS
CLOSE ENCOUNTERS OF THE DEADLY KIND
DEATH BY DEVIL'S FOOD
BLIND DATE'S BITTER END
THE TAVERNA AFFAIR
THE MUSIC BOX MYSTERY
TRUFFLES TO DIE FOR
COOKING SPIRITS
ADD A PINCH OF MURDER
SALSA AND SECRETS
DEADLY EVER AFTER